Slough Library Services

Please return this book on or before the date shown on your receipt.

To renew go to:
Website: **www.slough.gov.uk/libraries**
Phone: **03031 230035**

LIB/6198

WID

Slough
Borough Council
www.slough.gov.uk

SINGING RIVER

Whe— Sad Sontag and Swede Harrison stumble
upon the apparently lifeless body of "Sheep King"
Dan Reynolds in San Francisco, they flee the
hangman's noose to Singing River, Wyoming — a
place mentioned in a telegram in Reynolds's room.
But once they're taken on at the Two Bar J P, they
find themselves caught up in a war of sheepmen
versus cattlemen. Reynolds, needing more range for
his sheep, has a finger in every pie, and spies across
the land, including one at the Two Bar J P. Soon
Sad and Swede are suspected of working for the
sheepmen, while the recovering Reynolds is after
them for helping the cattlemen. Just about everyone
wants to capture or kill the two pards, it seems —
but when the bullets start to fly, they're determined
to stand their ground and see justice served.

D1339993

3013050566~

SPECIAL MESSAGE TO READERS

THE ULVERSCROFT FOUNDATION
(registered UK charity number 264873)
was established in 1972 to provide funds for
research, diagnosis and treatment of eye diseases.
Examples of major projects funded by
the Ulverscroft Foundation are:-

- The Children's Eye Unit at Moorfields Eye Hospital, London
- The Ulverscroft Children's Eye Unit at Great Ormond Street Hospital for Sick Children
- Funding research into eye diseases and treatment at the Department of Ophthalmology, University of Leicester
- The Ulverscroft Vision Research Group, Institute of Child Health
- Twin operating theatres at the Western Ophthalmic Hospital, London
- The Chair of Ophthalmology at the Royal Australian College of Ophthalmologists

You can help further the work of the Foundation
by making a donation or leaving a legacy.
Every contribution is gratefully received. If you
would like to help support the Foundation or
require further information, please contact:

THE ULVERSCROFT FOUNDATION
The Green, Bradgate Road, Anstey
Leicester LE7 7FU, England
Tel: (0116) 236 4325

website: www.foundation.ulverscroft.com

SINGING RIVER

W. C. TUTTLE

SAGEBRUSH
Large Print Westerns

First published in Great Britain by Collins
First published in the United States by Houghton Mifflin

First Isis Edition
published 2019
by arrangement with
Golden West Literary Agency

The moral right of the author has been asserted

Copyright © 1939 by W. C. Tuttle
Copyright © 1931 by W. C. Tuttle in the
British Commonwealth
Copyright © renewed 1967 by W. C. Tuttle
All rights reserved

A catalogue record for this book is available
from the British Library.

ISBN 978–1–78541–693–4 (pb)

Published by
F. A. Thorpe (Publishing)
Anstey, Leicestershire

Set by Words & Graphics Ltd.
Anstey, Leicestershire
Printed and bound in Great Britain by
T. J. International Ltd., Padstow, Cornwall

This book is printed on acid-free paper

CHAPTER
ONE

It was a wild night in the San Francisco Bay region. All shipping had been driven to cover, and the bay was a smother of pelting rain and scudding fog, as the wind howled in off the Pacific, whipping the old gray town of San Francisco with a steady blast.

Far up Market Street, protected from the elements by the doorway of a closed store and an awning, already whipped to shreds, stood two men. In daylight it would be noticed that one man was very tall, thin, with a long, serious cast of countenance, while the other was of medium height, of a decided Celtic type, broad of shoulder, bowed of legs. Their big Stetson hats, high-heeled boots and their peculiar stiff-legged walk would immediately brand them as a couple of boys from the cow country. Their "store clothes" did not fit so well, and their "boiled" collars had already worn red spots on their leathery necks.

"Jist like I said a while ago," remarked the shorter one, "Swede" Harrigan, "you ain't got a lick of sense, Sad. In this here thawed-out blizzard? Cowboy, you shore craves queer things."

"I was talkin' with that feller back there in that see-gar store," said "Sad" Sontag. "He said it was the

1

greatest sight yuh ever seen. Can yuh imagine the danged ocean pilin' in plumb up over them rocks? He says most everybody goes out to see the storm. Hell, there ain't nothin' wrong about my idea. And here's another thing, Swede. You like fish, dontcha?"

"Yeah, I like fish."

"All right. That feller said lotsa times the ocean gits so riled up that fish are throwed plumb out of the ocean. He said some fellers go out with them butterfly nets and catch 'em goin over. Jist reach up and — and the fish is yours."

"Cowboys," said Swede seriously, "ain't the only damn liars on earth."

"And anyway," commented Swede, after a long pause, "yuh couldn't see a fish six inches from yore nose on a night like this."

"Smell 'em," said Sad. "Smell 'em — and grab quick. I'll tell yuh what we'll do, and I'll pay for it. We'll take one of them taxicab things and go out to this here place he said — the — uh-h-h — Cliff House. He said that was the place to go and see it. How about yuh?"

"I ain't never seen no sea storm, Sad. Do yuh reckon that feller was a-lyin' about them fish?"

"We'll find out, if we can ever find one of them cabs."

They left their shelter and went skidding with the wind, aided and abetted by high heels, until they came to a panting rest around a corner, where they found a battered taxicab, drawn up out of the wind and rain. The grouchy driver surveyed them critically from beneath the brim of his dripping hat.

"Want to go out to the Cliff House?" he grunted. "Huh! Whole Pacific Ocean is comin' up over the cliffs right now. Helluva place to go!"

"You been out there to-night?" asked Swede.

"Made two trips out there in the fog."

"Didja see any fish?"

"Any what?"

"Fish!"

"What kinda fish?" The driver yelled.

"What kinda fish have they?"

"Git in!"

"Must have more'n one kind," said Sad, as the cab jerked ahead.

Lurching and skidding, they headed for the beach in the smother, and on Van Ness Street they lost a fender, which was apparently collected by a passing truck. But the driver did not seem to mind, except that it caused him to swear a little.

Up and down hill, around corners, their headlights making little illumination, the driver honking his horn in a desperate effort to prevent a head-on collision at corners. Then they were on a long, straight piece of pavement, and the taxi picked up speed against the wind.

"Hell of a night for fishin'," yelled Swede.

"For what?" yelled the driver, and the next instant another cab careened from a side street, going at a high rate of speed, and the two machines locked together, skidded across the street, and struck the curb with a splintering crash.

For several minutes there was no sound, except the wind and rain. Cars passed and repassed, never noticing the wrecked cabs against the gloom of a cut bank. Finally the voice of Sad Sontag, quavering a little:

"What the hell happened, anyway? Swede! Oh, Swede!"

"Hello yourself!"

Swede got up out of the wreckage, spat out some mud, and sloshed around in a muddy circle, like a dog getting ready to lie down. Sad grasped him by the arm.

"Are yuh hurt, pardner?" he asked.

"Hurt — hell! I'm mortified."

"What hit us?"

"I dunno," vaguely. "Mebbe it was a — a fish."

They laughed foolishly and began digging into the wreckage, where they discovered both drivers and two passengers. Their driver was conscious, but apparently in bad shape. The other driver and his two passengers were all unconscious. The two cowboys dragged them clear of the wreckage and after a number of failures, they managed to flag a passing machine. It was a big limousine, and the Japanese driver did not relish the task of taking the injured to the hospital; but Sad swore he'd throw him out and drive the machine himself, and the driver capitulated, said he would take them to the nearest hospital, and faded away in the gloom.

"Fish!" snorted Swede, wiping the mud off his face with a sleeve.

Sad laughed hollowly. "Guess we was lucky to sidestep the hospital."

"Wham! Man, didn't we take to that other machine? Lucky? Gosh, we must have been born with horse-shoes in our mouths! Well, I've lost my taste for fish, so we might as well go home."

4

"All right; which way is home?"

The debate was only half-hearted, neither of them being sure, so they started out. A few steps away from the wreck, Sad stopped suddenly. He had tripped over a pair of feet. It was another man, who had been flung in against the muddy bank, a dozen or more feet away from the wreck. Sad lighted a match, shielded it with his hat, and they looked down into the muddy face of a man, who had a gag between his teeth. His eyes were open, and he blinked in the light.

"Hands tied, too," grunted Swede. "Gimme yore knife, Sad."

Swiftly he cut away the ropes and removed the gag. The man was conscious. Mud and rain mixed with the blood from a cut cheek, as he sat up and flexed his muscles. One hand was bloody from a cut wrist, and his clothes were torn badly.

"Any bones busted?" asked Sad, as the man got to his feet, leaning on Swede for support.

"Guess not. That sure was a close call, boys. They had me on the floor, and when the crash came, I guess it flung a door open and I scooted out into the mud. Anyway, that must have been what happened. Now, the idea is to get home."

A pair of dim headlights appeared out of the gloom, a taxi-cab hugging the curb. The driver did not question their appearance, after his lights picked up the two smashed cabs. He merely asked where the rest of the accident had gone, and was told that they had been sent to the hospital.

"Been out to the beach?" asked Swede.

"Yep."

"See any fish?"

"Fish? Yea-a-ap. Lot of 'em, two-legged ones."

They sloshed down in the leather seat and headed back for town. The stranger was a big man, possibly fifty years of age, slightly gray, his eyes deep-set under bushy brows, broad nose and a wide, thin-lipped mouth above a fighting chin. Sad decided that the man had been powerful in his younger days, but soft living had put on a layer of fat and taken away muscles.

He had nothing to say about himself; why he had been bound and gagged, nor where they were taking him. And the two cowboys had lived their lives in the wide places of the West, where men do not ask questions. It was up to the man to tell them, if he cared for them to know.

Finally the cab drew up at a big house, the big man paid the fare, and they entered the house. It was a wonderful place, and the butler looked aghast at their appearance, muddy boots, muddy and torn clothing, dirty faces.

"Some whisky, Lee," said the big man brusquely, as he led the way into a gorgeously furnished library, where a fire crackled in the grate.

"Yes, sir. Pardon, sir, but there is a telegram on the table which came day before yesterday."

"All right, Lee; hurry the drinks."

The big man opened the telegram, and his face twisted grimly. He threw the telegram on the table, with a muttered curse, and came over to the fire.

6

"If you ever want anything done right — do it yourself," he said harshly. "Don't even trust your own flesh and blood. Damn young fool! Youth never understands. Whisky ruins 'em."

He turned and surveyed himself in a mirror. "Hell of a looking mess!"

"Yuh might have done worse," said Sad Sontag mildly.

"That's right! Worse? That wreck saved me from going over the rocks into the ocean to-night. Yes, I guess that was the plan. And here I am, hands free, able to enjoy my own liquor; while they are in the hospital or the morgue."

The butler came in with the glasses and liquor, which he placed on the table.

"Beg pardon, sir, but Mr. Gale just arrived," he said softly.

The big man had started to pour out the drinks, but lowered the decanter.

"Help yourselves, boys," he said, and walked out of the room.

Sad poured out the drinks, and the butler, after a glance at the fire, withdrew from the room. Sad swallowed his liquor and glanced at the open telegram. It was from Singing River, Wyoming, and read:

Gale got drunk and talked too much stop shipping him out ahead of possible trouble. — STEEN.

Sad came from the table and held a water-soaked boot near the blaze.

"This jigger must have plenty money," observed Swede. "I'll betcha yuh couldn't buy one of them there chairs for less'n twenty-five dollars apiece."

It would have shocked Swede had he known that the pair were bought at a forced sale for three thousand dollars.

"Make a swell bunk-house, eh?" laughed Sad.

"Never git any work out of a cowpuncher, if he lived like this. I'll be danged if I could ever understand why folks build big winders like them and then hang a lot of heavy stuff around 'em to keep out the sun."

"I dunno," replied Sad, "unless when yuh git a lot of money yuh become a sun dodger. I know danged well I —"

Sad stopped short. From somewhere in the house or just outside came the unmistakable sound of a shot, followed by another crash, as though something had fallen heavily on the floor.

Only for a moment did they hesitate, and then ran to the door, which opened into the hall. To the right was a huge living-room, subdued in lighting, through which came a blast of cold air and the acrid fumes of burned powder. Quickly they stepped into the room, noting a French door wide open, the draperies whipping in the wind. In front of the fireplace lay the big man, arms outspread, and near him on a Chinese rug lay a blued Colt revolver.

Sad picked it up and leaned down, looking at the big man. Over near the open door was a huge Chinese vase, which had been upset and broken. A hoarse sound caused them to whirl around, and there stood

8

the butler, white of face, staring at the man on the floor. His eyes lifted and he looked accusingly at Sad.

"My God, you've done for him, sir," he exclaimed.

Sad whirled quickly, the gun in his hand. The frightened butler's hands shot skyward, his heel caught on a rug, and down he went, upsetting a tall stand-lamp, which crashed down against a carved teak-wood table.

"Set 'em up in the other alley," choked Swede.

And as the dazed butler lifted his head above the wreckage, he saw the two cowboys disappearing through the open doorway. Quickly he got to his feet and ran to a telephone, while Sad Sontag and Swede Harrigan circled the house, climbed over an iron fence and went pounding down the foggy street.

"That jasper would send us both to meet a rope," panted Sad, as they halted at the corner of an old cemetery and waited for an approaching street car.

"You still got that gun?" asked Swede.

"Inside my shirt."

"Well, we're that much ahead, anyway."

They eventually reached the small lodging-house which had been home to them for a few days, and were warm and dry in their room. Swede was inclined to be amused over the whole thing.

"That's what a love for fish will lead to," he chuckled.

"That's right," thoughtfully, as Sad drew off a soggy boot. "Swede, yuh can see now how easy it is to convict an innocent man. That damn butler would swear we

9

shot that man. I'll betcha he could git up on a witness stand and describe jist how one of us shot him."

"Shore. Man, I'll never forget seein' that feller upset into that lamp, when yuh swung that six-gun toward him. I'll bet he felt himself over for bullet-holes."

The next morning at breakfast Sad had the feeling that the others at the table were looking at them curiously. Both of them carried a few visible bruises from the wreck, and Sad thought it might be the bruises which caused folks to look at them in that way. But after breakfast he happened to see the front page of a morning paper on the table.

Spread across the page was the glaring headline:

SHEEP KING SHOT DOWN BY COWBOYS.

Following the heading was a vivid tale of the shooting, as told by Henry Lee, the butler, and a fairly accurate description of Sad and Swede. The Sheep King's name was Dan Reynolds. The butler said that Mr. Reynolds had not been home for two days, until he came in out of the storm with the two cowboys. He said that all three men were muddy, wet and bloody. Mr. Reynolds had ordered him to bring some liquor, and that everything seemed peaceful. After serving the drinks he had retired from the room for several moments, when he heard the shot.

Running to the door of the living-room, he saw one of the cowboys, gun in hand, looking down at Reynolds. The cowboy whirled on him, threatening to shoot, and the butler caught his foot on a rug and fell.

He said the two cowboys disappeared through a French doorway, leaped off the porch and made their escape in the storm.

The story went on to say that the police easily verified the butler's story, and every avenue of escape was blocked, unless the two men were out of the country before the alarm had become general.

Up in their room, Sad related what the paper had said.

"We're jist in a hell of a hot place," said Sad. "That frozen-faced butler shore described us fine, and his testimony might hang both of us. Now I know where there's a second-hand clothin' store. You stay here, while I go out and buy somethin' we'll need."

Sad left his big hat in the room, and in fifteen minutes he was back with a package, which contained two pairs of well-worn shoes, two nondescript hats, two black coats, and two pairs of trousers, which did not match the coats. Swede paid their bill at the office, and fifteen minutes later they walked out, so altered in appearance that their best friends would not recognise them.

They realised that the ferries would be watched, and it seemed hours before they reached the Oakland side. They kept apart on the boat, and at the ticket office in Oakland, when Sad stepped up to purchase tickets, a uniformed officer sauntered in close.

"Where to?" queried the clerk.

Sad swallowed heavily. He could feel the officer looking at the back of his neck.

"To — uh — Singin' River, Wyomin'," said Sad thickly. "Two of 'em."

"Two tickets?"

"Yeah, I — I'm takin' my aunt with me."

It required some time for the clerk to make out the ticket, and Sad was relieved to find the officer gone. He found Swede, wig-wagged him a signal, and they went to their train, sitting apart until the train started, when Swede sighed heavily and sat down beside him.

"Where in hell are we goin'?" queried Swede.

"Singin' River, Wyomin'" whispered Sad hoarsely.

"Why?" in amazement.

"I dunno. There was a doggoned officer right behind me, and all I could think of was the address on that telegram last night — so I — I had to say somethin'. We had to go somewhere, cowboy."

"Yeah, that's right. Say! Did that paper say Reynolds was killed?"

"It said he was dangerously hurt."

"Shucks, yuh can't kill a shepherd. What was that telegram, Sad?"

"Somethin' about a feller named Gale gettin' drunk and talkin' too much, and shippin' him out ahead of trouble. It was signed Steen."

"Sounds interestin'. Singing River might be all right."

"Right or wrong, that's where we're goin', pardner. Anythin' sounds better to me than a judge and jury."

12

CHAPTER
TWO

Bill Steen, the big, blond, square-headed foreman of the Two Bar J P, leaned across his rough desk in the little office and frowned at the sandy-haired, freckled nosed Johnny Caldwell, whose blue eyes glared rather defiantly at the foreman. Johnny was of medium height and built like a middleweight fighter.

"Quittin', eh?" grunted Steen. "What's wrong with you?"

"Nothin' wrong with me," said Johnny evenly. "I've been ridin' that rim for months, and I've kept m' eyes open. Miss Proctor expects me to keep m' eyes open. But, Steen, I'll be damned if I ride any rim with men that don't keep awake."

"Meanin'?" queried Steen.

"Buck Welty. Yesterday I finds him asleep, with a bottle of liquor. I've found him off the job a dozen times in the last month. I'm through. I've tried to earn m' salt, and I'll be damned if I'm goin' to take the blame if anythin' goes wrong. I told Dell Rios about it, and he jist the same as told me to mind my own business. That's all right, too. If Dell Rios don't consider that rim ridin' worth anythin' to him, why don't he quit payin' a man to do his share of the ridin'?"

"I'm not runnin' Dell Rios' end of this game, Caldwell," coldly.

"You're responsible to Miss Proctor."

"Not for what Dell Rios does."

"Like hell, yo're not! Suppose them sheep outfits comes boilin' in over the rim. Yo're not responsible, eh?"

"If Rios is satisfied —"

"I'm not workin' for Rios, Steen. I don't mind tellin' yuh that I took a wallop at Welty and knocked him kickin'. He comes up with a gun in his hand and blood in his eye; so I pistol-whipped him plenty, and packed him home on his own bronc. I told Rios what I done, and I told Rios if he didn't like it —"

"You prob'ly would," dryly. "Lemme see how much you've got comin'."

"Thirty bucks — and I don't owe anybody."

"Johnny Caldwell, are you quitting me?"

Both men turned quickly to see Jean Proctor in the doorway. Jean Proctor was twenty-three, tall, slender, with hair as black as the proverbial raven's wing, and a skin as white as milk. Her features were as clean cut as a cameo, and her dark eyes seemed to mirror her every mood. Jean Proctor looked like a princess, worked like a cowboy, and swore like the devil, when the occasion demanded.

Johnny flushed quickly and shifted his hat from one hand to the other.

"Yes'm, I — I'm quittin'," he said softly. Johnny's one great dream had been to marry Jean Proctor, but he had never come nearer than calling her Jean. Everyone called her Jean.

"Why are you quitting me?" she asked. "Tired of the job?"

"No, ma'am," quickly. "I ain't tired of it. But like I was tellin' Bill; I don't like —"

"I heard what you told Bill. I appreciate the fact that you are working for my interests, and I quite agree with you that Dell Rios — Bill, does Rios know that Welty sleeps on the job?"

"I'm shore I don't know," smiled Steen.

"Well, he's damn soon going to know!" Jean's eyes flashed angrily. "If Dell Rios thinks for a minute that the rim is a bedroom, it's time he found out that it isn't. If he wants to get sheeped out, that's his business — but I don't."

"I'll speak to Dell about it."

"I already spoke to him," said Johnny dryly. "He said he supposed I'd come up here and tell you all about how lax he's been. It's thisaway, Miss Proctor; I've either got to watch all that rim alone, or I've got to pistol whip all of Rios' hired hands, until I git one that ain't so sleepy he can watch his own end of the rim. I ain't lookin' for trouble, and I can sleep as long as any puncher that ever rolled under a blanket, but I ain't goin' to lay down and let the sheep in on yuh."

Jean sighed and walked over to a window, where she looked out at the rambling buildings of the Two Bar J P. To the north stretched the rim, and to the south was the green ribbon, marking the course of the Singing River. Cattle bawled down at the old corrals, where several cowboys were branding calves, and through the open window came the smell of burning hair, the pungent odour of dust from the corral. The two men watched her silently, and finally she turned, her dark eyes sombre.

"I don't want you to quit, Johnny," she said, and walked out.

Steen grimaced and shook his head, looking inquiringly at Johnny, who looked at the doorway, blue eyes thoughtful. Then —

"If I kill a few of 'em, Bill — mebbe I can convince 'em that they ort to stay awake on the rim."

And Johnny Caldwell walked out, rattled his spurs down over the steps, and Steen saw him climb up on the corral fence to watch the branding. He saw Jean go down there, wearing her riding clothes, and she stopped at the fence. Johnny climbed down quickly. Jean knew he had not quit, because she would have had to sign his cheque.

"Thank you, Johnny," she said. "I need men I can trust."

"Thank yuh for sayin' that," he replied, flushing redly.

"It's true that I need men I can trust. I heard the other day that Reynolds is getting desperate. The feed and water are playing out in the Sunrise Hills. But as long as I've got twenty loyal men, he never can get into this valley."

16

"No, ma'am, he shore can't. And yuh don't need that many. I could take six good shots and stop him — if we know in time, ma'am." Johnny's face grew red and he fumbled with his hat. "I — I heard some things about Gale Arnold, and I — I — well, it ain't none of my business, but —"

Jean turned away and looked down the valley for several moments, and her lips were drawn in a hard line when she turned back.

"He is Reynolds' son," she said.

"That's what I heard."

"Let's forget him, Johnny."

"Yes'm — we shore will."

But Johnny wasn't so sure. Handsome Gale Arnold, the young millionaire from New York, who had wanted to learn the cattle business. Not from a desk, but from the deck of a broncho. He had met Bill Steen in Singing River, learned that Bill was foreman of the big Two Bar J P outfit, and put the proposition up to Bill.

Jean Proctor looked at Gale Arnold and smiled. And Gale was entirely "sold" on the Two Bar J P.

"Why do you want to learn the cattle business?" asked Jean.

"Because the life appeals to me," replied Gale.

"Just why did you select Singing River, Mr. Arnold?"

"I suppose the name appealed to me, Miss Proctor. I do not want any salary, but I do want to be treated the same as you treat your cowboys. My money has nothing to do with it at all."

And Gale Arnold was accepted on that basis. Johnny Caldwell looked him over and grew morose. Gale had everything that Johnny lacked; good-looks, education and money. Johnny was only a rim rider, a rough, tough fighter with either gun or fists. He could read and write, roll a cigarette with either hand, ride any horse in the valley, and sing a reedy sort of tenor — limited to a few songs, of course.

Gale Arnold proceeded to fall in love with Jean Proctor, thereby losing much of his status as a cowboy, because it ruined what little efficiency he had left — or had acquired. But that was what he came there for. His job was to marry Jean Proctor, and it looked as though he would carry it through to a great success, except that a few drinks of highproof whisky on an empty stomach caused him to talk too much.

The news that Gale Arnold was Gale Reynolds, son of the Sheep King, was a shock to Jean Proctor, but she took it without flinching. Bill Steen happened to be in Singing River with Gale the night he told who he really was, and Bill proceeded to ship Gale west on the first train. Steen knew what would happen if Gale ever went back to the Two Bar J P; the boys would kill him, and no jury in the county would convict them.

Jean Proctor did not wear her heart on her sleeve, and no one knew how she felt about it. Her eyes clouded at the mention of Gale's name, but she made no comments on what he had done to her.

"Why'nt yuh let the pole-cat come back here, Bill?" asked Curley Adams, a horse wrangler. "I'd like to run our brand on his damn belly and send him home to his pa."

And the rest of the crew nodded. It would have been a pleasure. They idolized Jean Proctor, and a hurt to her was a hurt to them. Every man of them wanted to pat her on the back and tell her it was good riddance to bad rubbish, but they lost their nerve and grew tongue-tied.

Singing River, in spite of being the county seat and the biggest shipping point in that part of the country, had never outgrown its cowtown appearance and manners. The river itself barely reached the town, where it sank far beneath the surface. North of the town, down through the range of the Two Bar J P, Circle R, and the Bar 44, it ran a sizeable stream, furnishing plenty of water, grassy bottoms and cottonwood and willow shade. South of the town was a vast stretch of desert country, unwatered, controlled by the Flying M outfit, who had been obliged to sink deep wells, which barely pumped enough water for their stock.

Dan Reynolds had looked upon the north range of Singing River and saw a wonderful land for ranging his sheep. His vast range, farther to the north, far beyond the encircling rim, which guarded the north end of the Singing River range, was played out. Thousands of sheep, year after year, had made dust-heaps of the once grassy hills.

Reynolds had to have more range, and he needed it now. He had tried to make a deal with old Jim Proctor, who died and left the Two Bar J P to Jean. He tried to make a deal with old Hewie Moore, owner of the Bar 44, and with Dell Rios, owner of the Circle R. But they

19

were sheep haters, scorning any offer he might make. They only owned outright a small percentage of the range they controlled, but possession was nine points in the law. With the rim to guard them, patrolled by keen-eyed cowboys, and with the grassless country below them, they felt fairly secure.

"There'll be traitors," declared "Uncle Hewie." "We've got to expect things like that; but when we git one — he hangs. Dan Reynolds will never sheep out this range — not before my eyes. Jim Proctor guarded that old rim for years, and Jean ain't the kind to ever lay down on the job."

"Stormy" See had been foreman for Uncle Hewie, until the voters of the valley decided that Stormy would make a good sheriff. Stormy was of medium height, angular, bony, roan haired. His pointed nose was inclined to redness, his eyes rather pessimistic.

Stormy appointed "Tiny" Parker as deputy sheriff. Tiny was a two hundred and forty pound cowboy, moon-faced, addicted to guitar music, and with a sense of humour which seemed to appal Stormy, who needed a diagram to see the point of a joke.

Stormy was single, a confirmed bachelor, while Tiny had married a Swedish girl, a short, blonde, fat little lady, who spoke English with a decided accent, and whose sense of humour was nearly as pronounced as Stormy's. She believed implicitly in Tiny, who lied to her all the time; for no purpose, except, as he said, to keep in practice.

Stormy was sitting, half-asleep at his office desk, feet higher than his head, while Tiny tried clumsily to splice a broken E-string on his old guitar. Buddy Fowler, aged five, the son of the blacksmith, sat on the steps of the office, watching Tiny. Buddy had a moon-like little face and wide blue eyes, golden hair and a wide grin.

"You go play music?" asked Buddy innocently. Tiny looked up, his face red from suppressing the oaths that welled up within him against the guitar string.

"Yeah, I reckon I'll do a couple yards of music, if I ever git fixed," he replied.

"I like it," said Buddy. Tiny opened his mouth in a soundless laugh and looked at Stormy.

"The kid's got a ear for music," grunted Stormy.

"With a Swedish viewpoint," grinned Tiny, and began tightening the string carefully, his brows lifted in anticipation of a sudden snap.

"Rios loadin' t'day, ain't he?" queried Stormy.

Tiny nodded cautiously. "Bunch of white-faced steers. Burrs in their tails and fire in their eyes. Man, I'll betcha they've lived all their lives on the rim. Knocked down half the loadin' corral, and they're holdin' part of the bunch outside. They're jist like a danged bunch of buffalo."

Tiny twanged the string softly. A man came in and handed the sheriff a telegram, grinned at Tiny and spoke to little Buddy as he went out. He was Ed. Wilmer, the depot agent, who delivered his own telegrams. The sheriff opened the telegram and read it carefully.

Watch for two cowboys named Sontag and Harrigan wanted here for shooting of Dan Reynolds stop bought

tickets for your town stop advise me if they show up. —
CARRIGAN, Chief of Detectives.

Stormy handed the wire to Tiny, who read it carefully.

"Ain't been no strangers in here," said Tiny. "And if
there had —"

"I didn't know Dan Reynolds had been shot, did
you?"

"If he has — fine. Yuh don't think I'm goin' to put on
any crape, do yuh? And as far as them two
cowpunchers are concerned —"

"A shootin' is a shootin'," said Stormy. "The law
don't take yore occupation into consideration.

"That's all right. But you better lay off them big
words. Some day you'll sprain a tonsil and talk with a
accent all the rest of yore life, Stormy."

Came the whistle of a locomotive, and Stormy
looked at his watch. The passenger was on time. Little
Buddy got up and went toddling up the sidewalk.
Stormy went to the doorway. From there he could see
the depot, and he saw Sontag and Harrigan leave the
train and start down the street. He did not know it was
them, but his guess was correct.

"They've done showed up," he told Tiny, who came
to the doorway and looked up the street.

From the opposite direction came a wild cowboy
yell, and they turned to see twenty or thirty wild-eyed,
white-faced steers break into the street and head
toward the depot, while in through an alley raced two
perspiring cowboys, jumping their horses across the
sidewalk in a mad effort to turn the steers.

22

A woman in front of a store screamed a warning, and the sheriff sprang out of the doorway. Little Buddy had started across the street, heading for his father's blacksmith shop, square in the path of those wild-running steers. They had bunched, running in a cloud of dust. Instinctively the sheriff jerked up his left arm, covering his face. He loved every inch of that little toddler.

The maddened steers were twenty feet away and little Buddy had stopped, facing the steers, the wind ruffling his thatch of golden hair. Suddenly a lean form hurtled out from the sidewalk with a pantherish leap. Another long leap and he hand-reached the boy. Swinging him low, he sent the little fellow skidding and rolling out of the path of the slashing hoofs. For a moment he seemed engulfed by the herd, then he came into sight.

"Ride 'im, cowboy!" screamed a voice.

Out of the broken herd came a single animal, whirled around, with the cowboy fastened to its neck. Down went the steer and man in a crashing heap, but the steer regained its feet, head down, seemed to tear loose and went galloping blindly away. Slowly the tall cowboy got to his feet, a grin on his dusty face.

Men were running toward him, as he staggered to the sidewalk, trying to fill his lungs with air. One shirt sleeve was badly torn, his vest hanging to one shoulder. The sheriff was the first man to reach him.

"Hurt?" asked Stormy.

Sad shook his head, unable to speak. Swede Harrigan was hammering him on the back. Little

Buddy was watching them curiously, blinking dust from his eyes. And here was Fowler, the big blacksmith, his tongs in hand, his face white beneath the grime.

"Gawd!" he choked. "I seen it. I tell yuh, I seen it. They'd 'a' killed my boy. Nothin' on earth could 'a' saved him — nothin'!"

He picked the boy up in his brawny arms, hugging him tightly, and Buddy, taking his cue from this, began crying too. Sad managed to gather enough breath to assure them that he was all right. Tiny took Sad's hand and gripped it tightly.

"Darn steer got one horn through the sleevehole of my vest," grinned Sad. "We shore went around a few, didn't we?"

"Never mind the vest; I'll buy yuh a hundred," said the blacksmith.

"And I'll pay for half of 'em," grinned the sheriff.

Sad grinned at Buddy's tear-streaked face.

"Did I hurt yuh any, pardner?" he asked, and Buddy shook his head.

"That's great. You shore slide well for a youngster. Well, I reckon I better find a hotel where I can clean up a little."

"Jist across the street," said Tiny, pointing. "I'll go with yuh."

Stormy watched them cross the street, thought it over for several moments. Finally he walked up to the depot, asked for a telegraph blank, on which he wrote:

"Carrigan, Detective Department, San Francisco, Calif.

"No sign of men mentioned in your telegram stop probably bought ticket to throw you off right trail."

SEE, Sheriff.

The depot agent checked over the words, and looked up at Stormy.

"There was a couple strange cowboys in on the train a bit ago."

"Strangers — hell!" snorted Stormy. "Them two are friends of mine."

The agent looked quizzically at Stormy. He had known the sheriff for several years and felt privileged.

"Old friends, Stormy?" he asked.

"No-o-o, not so old. Oldest one ain't much over thirty."

The sheriff sauntered around to the loading corrals. He wanted to warn the boys to hold those wild steers off the street. Not that they were not doing their best, but because Stormy wanted a chance to work off steam. He found Jeff Ellis, Rios' foreman, helping with the loading.

"Keep them steers off the main street, Jeff," he ordered. "Bunch of 'em damn near killed a little kid a while ago."

"We're havin' a tough time," admitted Ellis. "They smashed the corral on us."

"Where's Dell Rios?"

"He ain't here, Stormy."

"Out at the ranch?"

"No-o-o, he's out of the valley for a few days. Kinda took a run out to the Coast. Been gone four, five days

25

now. Ort to be back soon. Didja want him for anythin' in particular?"

"Oh, no, nothin' particular, Jeff. I jist heard that Dan Reynolds got shot a few days ago."

"Dead?"

"Dunno."

Jeff chewed a straw reflectively. "What didja think about young Reynolds?"

"That dirty coyote! I tell yuh, Jeff, Reynolds wouldn't stop at anythin' to get that Two Bar J P. The idea of that son of his masqueradin' as Gale Arnold, of New York. Supposin' he did marry Jean. She'd find out who he was, and cut him off at the pockets. Did he think he'd control things enough to let his old man come in over the rim?"

"Lotsa funny things might happen, Stormy."

"Yeah, that's right."

"Well, I've got to load a lot of steers before dark."

Stormy wandered back to his office, where he found Tiny.

"Well, Old Law and Order," said Tiny, "them is yore two men. They done introduced themselves to me."

"You never said nothin' about that telegram, didja?"

"What telegram?"

They looked at each other closely and with understanding.

"Huh!" grunted Stormy. "I must 'a' been kinda dreamin' to myself."

"Ever once in a while yuh do. Mild form of insanity."

Stormy grinned and went back to his desk.

CHAPTER
THREE

Tiny Parker's bump of curiosity was prominent. He wanted to talk about the sheep situation and about Reynolds to Sad and Swede and see what they had to say and how they acted. Tiny had an idea he was able to read expressions, but was disappointed in what he read in the faces of these two strange cowboys. The name of Reynolds failed to cause them uneasiness, so Tiny settled down to his job and told them much of the valley history.

"And that girl runs the Two Bar J P, eh?" said Sad.

"As good as her father did. She's plumb capable."

"And almost married into sheep," grinned Swede.

"That's right."

"Who owns this big Flyin' M?" asked Sad.

"Feller named Farraday, I think. They're a wild bunch of cactus jumpers down there. When they have a pay day, we set tight. Salty as the ocean, that gang."

"This Proctor girl must have good men workin' for her."

"Best on earth. Bill Steen is the foreman, and Bill is a dinger."

"Yea-a-ah?" Sad figuratively pricked up his ears. "They've got to guard against sheep all the time, eh?"

"Shore, against Dan Reynolds' outfit. The Two Bar J P keep two men on the rim, the Circle R, one man, and the Bar 44 keep one man. Gives 'em four good men up there — four good sheep haters."

"They'd have to be," said Sontag. "They'd have to be men that yo're sure about."

"They are, Sontag; the pick of the outfits."

It was about noon when Jean Proctor drove into town, with her team of matched bays, hitched to a spring-wagon. She scorned the idea of having one of the boys drive her team. It seemed to Jean that everybody in town tried to tell her about the man saving the life of little Buddy Fowler. They told it from hearsay, several times removed, many different versions and variations. Even Fowler left his shop to tell her about it. Little Buddy was a great favourite, and Sad was in grave danger of having the main street renamed Sontag avenue.

She met Tiny Parker with Sad and Swede, and Tiny hastened to introduce them. The depot agent had already told her that Sontag and Harrigan were old friends of Stormy See.

"I've heard a lot about you," she told Sad.

"Oh, yea-a-ah, about me and the steer wearin' the same vest," laughed Sad.

"I didn't hear about the vest part of it."

"That was the comedy end of the thing," grinned Swede.

"I suppose. But it was a mighty brave thing to do, Mr. Sontag. You see, if anything happened to Buddy, we'd lose a lot of sunshine around this town. We all

28

seem to have sort of a claim on Buddy. His mother died when he was only a few weeks old, and we've all loved him to death."

"Pretty lucky kid," sighed Swede.

"To have his mother die?"

"No — to have you all lovin' him."

Jean flushed a little. "Anyway," holding out her hand to Sad, "I am glad to have met you, Mr. Sontag."

She shook hands with Swede and entered a store.

"By golly, if that's a sample of this country — I'm stayin'," declared Swede. "Didja ever see such eyes and such skin? And you, a hero in her eyes," he said, looking malevolently at Sad. "I allus git the worst of it."

"You've still got both arm-holes in yore vest," grinned Sad, "And there's plenty more wild steers."

"Yea-a-ah! I'd prob'ly lose m' pants. Let's git a drink."

Jean Proctor met Stormy See in the post office, and he started to tell her the story all over again.

"I've heard it seven different ways, and I've met the man himself," she told Stormy, laughing.

"Thasso? Anyway, it was great."

"It certainly was. They tell me that Sontag and Harrigan are old, old friends of yours, Stormy."

"Well, yea-a-ah," thoughtfully.

"They seem like a nice pair of men."

"Finest yuh ever knew."

"I'm glad to hear you say that, because I can use two more men. You see, I wanted to get your opinion before I asked them if they needed work. Now, I shall not be afraid to take them to the ranch."

"Well — uh — yeah."

Stormy watched her walk away, cuffed his hat over one eye and wondered just how big a fool he really was. He knew nothing about them. They were total strangers in Singing River, and any man, woman or child knew as much about them as he did. Still, he had recommended them.

"Wanted in Frisco for shootin' a man — and here I — oh, hell!"

Stormy bow-legged his way down to the office, hitting his heels hard on the old wooden sidewalk.

Jean met Sad and Swede in front of a store a few minutes later.

"If you two boys are looking for work, I can use you," she said. "I just had a talk with Stormy See, the sheriff, about you, and he recommends you highly."

"Well, that's mighty nice of yuh, ma'am," said Swede quickly. "We're shore in the market for a pair of jobs."

"Then that is settled. I shall be ready to go back in about fifteen minutes."

Jean entered the store and the two cowboys stared at each other.

"Stormy recommended us," said Sad. "How could he?"

"Never look at a gift horse's teeth," replied Swede. "C'mere!" Grasping Sad's sleeve. "You danged fool, you'd go in and tell her there must be some mistake. You and me have got to buy a few things for the ranch work."

Jean insisted on driving her own team. They stopped at the ranch-house of the Circle R, the Rios outfit, and Jeff Ellis came out to them.

"I want to speak with Dell Rios," she told him.

"Dell ain't here now, Miss Proctor; he took a trip out to the coast, and he ort to be back pretty soon. Anythin' I can do for yuh?"

"I'd rather see Dell about it," she replied. "But maybe you can fix it up some way. It's about Buck Welty."

"Oh, yea-a-ah. Him and Johnny Caldwell had a run-in."

"Johnny says Buck slept on the job."

"Uh-huh, and Buck says he didn't."

Jean's eyes flashed angrily. "I believe Johnny."

"I know yuh do, and we believe Buck. But, shucks, what's the use? Yuh don't need to worry about the rim. Punchers are always quarrellin'. Buck is pretty salty, and Johnny ain't no milk-drinkin' pale-face. They're both good men, Miss Proctor — and yuh need good men."

"The Circle R needs good men as badly as I do."

"I know we do. I'll speak to Dell when he gits back. I know he don't want anybody quarrellin' up there."

"Thank you, Ellis."

Jean did not think to introduce Sad and Swede to the foreman of the Circle R. After they left the ranch Jean told them something of the range history of Singing River. She mentioned her father's death, and Sad asked about it.

"He has been dead nearly a year now," she replied sadly. "It happened in that corral near the Circle R ranch-house. Dad was down there with Bill Steen, our foreman, looking at some horses. He and Bill and Ellis were in the corral together. Dad always was so careful around wild stock, but this time —"

"Horse kicked him?" asked Sad.

Jean nodded and busied herself with the lines.

"I've had to run the ranch since then," she said. "Running it at a loss."

"At a loss?" queried Sad.

Jean nodded, her eyes fixed on the horses.

"Rustlers?"

She smiled grimly. "Horses and cattle are not in the habit of going away of their own free will, are they, Mr. Sontag?"

"I never knowed any to do that," admitted Sad seriously. "How about the other ranchers at this end of the valley?"

"You talk with Uncle Hewie Moore the first time you get a chance. He owns the Bar 44. You'll like him. Uncle Hewie talks less and says more, when he's sober, than any man in the valley."

"Likes his little drink, eh?"

"Adores it. Aunt Ida, his wife, breathes temperance, quotes the Bible and sings hymns."

"Sort of a martyr, eh?"

"Martyr? Not much, she ain't. She lands on Hewie like a ton of brick, every time he gets drunk. And there is old Judge Pennington. Every time those two get together, they both get disgraceful. Of course, he isn't a judge, it is merely a nickname. Uncle Hewie has little education, and I believe the Judge has less."

"Miss Proctor, has Reynolds ever made you an offer for yore ranch?" asked Sad. "I heard a lot about the sheep trouble, and I wondered if he ever tried to buy out this end of the valley."

"He never made me an offer. Several times he tried to buy out dad, but dad refused. There isn't money enough on earth to have induced dad to allow sheep up here. He loved cattle and horses, and he swore that no sheep could ever come in over the rim."

"Hurrah for him!" snorted Swede.

"I don't reckon Reynolds would fight fair," said Sad.

"No," said Jean coldly. "Reynolds will not fight fair; he's got too much at stake. His range is gone. It's root hog or die with him now. I've seen it coming a long time."

"Are you afraid?"

"Not as long as I know I have loyal men."

"Are yuh sure, Miss Proctor?"

Jean nodded quickly, glancing curiously at Sad.

"Why do you ask that?"

"It's a good thing to be sure," said Sad.

Jean watched the road for quite a stretch, finally turning to Sad.

"I don't like the way you asked that question," she said. "You are a stranger in this country, know little of conditions and people, and yet you ask me if I am sure my men are loyal. No, it is not the mere asking of that question, but — well, the way you asked it."

Sad smiled at her and shook his head. "I reckon yuh misconstrued my tone of voice, Miss Proctor."

"Perhaps," said Jean dryly.

The Two Bar J P was a typical old cattle ranch. The buildings were all low, rambling, part log, part-lumber.

33

The ranch-house was a comfortable, rambling old affair, with beamed ceilings, fireplaces, wide porches. It was crudely furnished, but comfortable and picturesque. The bunk-house would easily accommodate a dozen men, the bunks built in against both walls.

Bill Steen, the foreman, was at the ranch. Sad noted that Bill was not so pleased over Jean hiring two strangers, and Jean probably noted it, too, because she explained that these men were old friends of Stormy See, and that Stormy recommended them. Steen was a big, burly, square-headed sort of a blond, with eyes the colour of blue in ice.

"You'll have to furnish ridin' rigs," said Sad.

"All right," growled Steen. "We've got plenty. Saddle room down there at this end of the stable. Pick out what yuh like. I'll have a wrangler bring in the remuda in the mornin', and yuh can pick yore string. Yuh won't need more than a couple apiece, 'cause the work ain't heavy now.

"Fact of the matter is, I dunno what in hell Jean hired yuh for. We've got more men now than we've got work for. But that's like a woman."

"Mebby she wanted a couple *good* men," said Swede innocently.

Steen digested this slowly.

"Didja hear that Dan Reynolds got shot?" asked Sad.

"Reynolds got shot?" parroted Steen. "Who shot him?"

"I dunno."

"Yuh mean somebody killed him?"

"I didn't say they killed him. The sheriff's office got the report."

"Well I'll be danged!"

Sad and Swede went down and selected their saddles and bridles, made stirrup adjustments and selected lariats from a number on the wall. After they were finished they met Steen at the bunk-house.

"Didja stop at the Rios place on the way out?" he asked.

"Yeah, we stopped there," replied Sad.

"See Rios?"

"No, he wasn't there. Gone to the Coast for a few days."

"Yea-a-a-ah? Gone to the Coast, eh?"

"That's what a feller named Jeff told Miss Proctor."

"Uh-huh. You fellers pick out any two bunks that ain't in use. You'll find plenty blankets. Yuh better fill up them strawticks, they ain't been filled for quite a while."

"Do you know Reynolds?" asked Sad.

"No, I don't know him — and I don't want to know the dirty shepherd."

Sad watched Steen go striding toward the ranch-house, and turned to Swede.

"There must be another Steen in this country, pardner."

"Looks thataway."

"Well, let's pick out our bunks."

CHAPTER
FOUR

A week at the Two Bar J P gave Sad a good chance to get acquainted with everyone and everything around the ranch. Stormy and Tiny rode out a couple of times to see how things were going. Stormy was worried over his recommendations, but things seemed to be going smoothly.

Sad and Swede had been up on the rim and had met Johnny Caldwell, and Slim Reed, the two men from the Proctor outfit, Buck Welty, from the Circle R, and Tony Rush, from the Bar 44. Sad liked Johnny instinctively. Slim was an easygoing cowboy, letting Johnny set the pace. Rush was a cynical sort, a confirmed sheep hater. Sad was unable to quite figure Buck Welty. He seemed pleasant enough, but there seemed to be a sarcastic note about his remarks, and his eyes seemed to harden every time he looked at Johnny Caldwell.

Sad knew that Johnny had given Welty a severe beating just a short time before Sad and Swede arrived in the valley, which might account for Welty's feelings toward the freckled-nosed, blue-eyed cowboy. The four men bunked in a shack on the rim, taking turns with the cooking. The work was easy; too easy, perhaps.

Welty loved liquor, and it would be easy for him to get it.

Johnny Caldwell rode back with them. He needed clean clothes, and there were no facilities for washing up there on the rim. Sad quizzed him about Welty, and Johnny was willing to talk about him.

"Me and him had a run-in a while back, and I whipped him plenty. He's all mouth and no ability. Yuh see, Sontag, up there on the rim, we've got nothin' to do, except to ride and look. There's plenty spots where yuh can see a long ways down into the sheep country. If the wind is right, yuh can smell 'em. It would take ten, twelve hours for anybody to send a bunch of sheep out of the valley and over the rim. There's two good passes to come through, and four men could hold either pass — it they had enough warnin'.

"Our job is to stay up there, spot anythin' like a drive, and — didja see that big stack of dry wood out there a hundred yards from the shack? There's five gallons of kerosene cached in that pile. Down on the edge of the rim is fifty pounds of dynamite, sealed up in the rocks. It's shore enough to wake folks up down the river, and that wood would shore make a good signal."

"Looks to me as though yuh was pretty well protected," said Swede.

Johnny nodded grimly. "Unless somethin' goes wrong."

"What sort of a fellow is Rios?" asked Sad.

"Dell is fine. At one time he kinda aimed to marry Jean, but she wasn't so keen about it, and her Dad didn't favour the idea a-tall. After the old man was killed, Dell kept on wantin' to marry her, but — well," Johnny smiled wistfully, "he didn't git very far with it. Dell's nice lookin', and he's a shore good cowman."

They got back to the ranch about the time Carey Poole, one of the Two Bar J P cowboys, came back from town. He had a newspaper story about the shooting of Dan Reynolds. It said that Reynolds was out of danger, and that he did not know who shot him. According to the newspaper, the police department were still trying to locate the two cowboys who were with Reynolds at the time of the shooting.

"Them two wasn't no cowboys," declared old Lightnin', the ranch-house cook. "No cowboys ever was with a shepherd. Prob'ly a couple herders that stole boots from a drunken waddy."

No one ever knew him by any other name. He was just Lightnin', age anywhere beyond sixty, weight a hundred and fifteen, height nearly six feet. According to Johnny Caldwell, "Lightnin' and Adam are the same age. Lightnin' can remember back to a time when there wasn't no wimmin. Part bob-cat, part wolf, drink his weight in whisky, and whip half the young men in the valley. And how he can mingle beans and biscuits!"

Years in the saddle had warped Lightnin's thin legs, until Swede said he felt that somebody ought to nail a brace between his knees. His sparse gray moustache fuzzed out like the whiskers on a bobcat, and his old eyes carried a wicked gleam at all times. He hated women, but the boys said he would sell his soul to the devil, if the payment would be of any benefit to Jean Proctor.

In one corner of his kitchen stood an old sawed-off ten gauge shot-gun, loaded with buckshot. Lightnin' never allowed anyone to touch it.

"Them shepherds might take the valley," he told Sad seriously, "but they'll never take this kitchen."

Jean called Johnny in the house and questioned him about Buck Welty.

"Oh, he's been actin' all right since I knocked down his ears," grinned Johnny. "Me and him ain't blendin' our voices in complete harmony, but he's actin' better."

"I'm glad of that," sighed Jean. "What do you think of the two new men?"

"Well, I dunno 'em well enough to pronounce any sentence on 'em," grinned Johnny, "but they shore seem to stack up great. That Sontag person is a great one to want to know things. He wanted to know all about how we'd signal down the valley, and all that."

"He wanted to know all that, did he?" thoughtfully. "I wonder why?"

"I suppose it's 'cause he's workin' for yuh and," Johnny paused for a moment, looking curiously at Jean. "You ain't thinkin' they might —"

Jean shook her head quickly. "They couldn't be connected with Reynolds and still be friends of Stormy See."

"No-o-o, that couldn't hardly be — but I'd kinda ask Stormy. He's been here a long time, and it stands to reason he ain't seen these boys for a long time. A — a feller might change, yuh know."

39

"That is true enough, Johnny. Steen seemed to think I was foolish to hire, them, but I — you heard about Sontag saving little Buddy Fowler?"

"Yes'm, I heard about it. That took nerve, y'betcha. If he ain't honest, he's got the lyin'est eyes on earth."

Jean nodded seriously. "I went down to see Dell Rios about Welty the day they came, and Dell had gone to the Coast for a few days."

"To Frisco," said Johnny. "I heard Welty mention it. Didja see the paper Poole brought in? It said that Reynolds was recoverin'. It seems that the police are huntin' for a couple cowboys who were with Reynolds. They prob'ly think they shot him. If they did, they ort to be sent to the pen."

"Why?" asked Jean quickly.

"For not doin' a good job of it."

"Johnny, you're bloodthirsty."

"Yes'm — where shepherds are concerned."

It seemed to Sad that Bill Steen was a bit concerned over Jean having a conference with Johnny Caldwell, and when Johnny came out, Steen tried to find out what had been said. But Johnny was calm-like. He took his clean clothes, stuffed them in his war-sack, and rode back to the rim.

The next day Stormy See came out to the ranch. The crew were all out on the range; so he sat down on the porch to talk with Jean. Stormy had another telegram from the detective bureau of San Francisco, in which he was notified to drop search for the two cowboys, as Reynolds had explained that these two men had nothing to do with the shooting.

40

The telegram bothered Stormy. It looked to him as though Sontag and Harrigan might be friends of Reynolds. If they were with Reynolds at Reynold's home, it stood to reason that they were not enemies of the big sheep-man. He hated to admit to Jean that he had lied about them being friends of his, because she might not understand how easily the mistake had been made. But Jean made it easier, when she said:

"Stormy, I've been wondering about Sontag and Harrigan."

"Yuh have?" quickly. "Wonderin' what?"

"Just how long since you knew them well."

Stormy cuffed his hat over one eye and looked at her.

"Jean, I'll tell yuh the truth — I never seen 'em in my life, until they hit Singin' River. Now, wait. Yuh can go ahead and cuss me, if yuh want to, but I've got to tell yuh how it happened. Sontag saved little Buddy Fowler. I seen that done. Right then I was backin' Sontag. Yuh see, I — I kinda like that little kid.

"Well, I'd had a telegram from San Francisco, askin' me to arrest Sontag and Harrigan, if they showed up here, for shootin' Dan Reynolds. Well, I hate sheep as bad as any livin' man, I reckon, but law is law; so I was goin' to arrest 'em both. But Sontag saved Buddy, and I wired San Francisco that they never showed up. The depot agent kinda horned in on the thing, him naturally havin' read the telegram; and I told him that the strangers was old, old friends of mine. That's how it started.

"The word got around awful quick, and I — I had to lie quite a lot. I lied to you, Jean. That is, about the friendship business. I figured that as long as they had shot Dan Reynolds, they'd be loyal to yore side. But now, I dunno so much about it."

"What changed your ideas?" asked Jean.

"Another telegram from Frisco, sayin' to drop search for them two cow-punchers, 'cause Reynolds said they was in his house that night, but had nothin' to do with the shootin'."

"What does that mean?" quickly.

Stormy shook his head. "I dunno. If they wasn't friends of Reynolds, what was they doin' in his house that night. Jean, I'm scared they're in here for Reynolds. We can't prove anythin'. I hate to believe what I feel about it. I never held myself up as a judge of human nature, but I'd 'a' backed them two anywhere. I reckon we jist live and learn."

"It seems that way, Stormy."

"I seen Dell Rios to-day; he's back from his trip, wearin' a big white Stetson and packin' a new silver mounted six-gun."

"Dell is inclined to be gaudy. But, Stormy, what would you advise me to do about Sontag and Harrigan?"

"Dog-gone, you've shore got me there, Jean. I dunno what to say."

"I suppose I better let them both go to-day."

"Do yuh know what I'd do, if I was you? I'd keep 'em on. Wouldn't say a word to Steen nor anybody. Kinda keep a check on both of 'em, and sooner or later they'll make a break — if they're Reynolds' men. As long as yuh suspect 'em, they can't do much. But don't let anybody else in on it. You know me — I keep still."

Jean smiled. "I know I can trust you, Stormy — and I'll take your advice."

"That's fine. But what made yuh so curious about 'em?"

"They were up on the rim, and Johnny Caldwell rode back with them. I had a private talk with Johnny, and he said Sontag asked a lot of questions about how they were to signal the valley in case of trouble — and all that."

Stormy shut his lips tightly and bobbed his head knowingly.

"The evidence kinda piles up agin 'em, Jean. But I'd wait. Right now, we don't *know* a thing. They're cowboys in every movement, but a cowboy might turn toward sheep — for a price."

For the next several days they were busy moving a bunch of several hundred head of steers to the south end of the range, and range branding calves. Both Sad and Swede were adept calf ropers, and Steen had given them both good roping horses and saddles.

Sad and Swede met Dell Rios, and were rather impressed by the owner of the Circle R. Dell Rois was a big, husky man of about twenty-five, almost as dark as an Indian, handsome of feature, picturesque of garb. Sad studied Steen and Rios together, and he mentally decided that the two men were not exactly friends. Rios' eyes held a cynical glint, while Steen seemed to watch Rios stolidly.

Sad, Swede and Carey Poole stopped at the Bar 44 and met Uncle Hewie Moore and his wife, known locally as Aunt Ida. Uncle Hewie was a little man, as gray as a rabbit, thin, wiry, with clear gray eyes and a high-pitched voice; one of the old type of cattlemen. Aunt Ida would weigh about two hundred and thirty, stood head and shoulders above Uncle Hewie, and believed implicitly in the heated hereafter for sinners. Aunt Ida was vast physically, but as Carey Poole, an Arizona-born cowboy said, "not so dern wide mentally."

"Do you drink?" she asked Swede confidentially.

"Well," grinned Swede, "now that yuh mention it, Mrs. Moore, I don't mind a snifter."

Uncle Hewie cuffed his hat clear across the room and let out a whoop of joy, while his wife glared at him malevolently.

"He-he-he thought yuh was offerin' him some, Idy!" exploded Hewie.

Quiet was finally restored, but not until Hewie went out and hung over a corral fence, trying to control his unholy mirth.

"You knew I was not offering you a drink, Mr. Harrigan," said Aunt Ida indignantly. "You know I wouldn't do a thing like that."

"Well, I've drunk with some awful good folks," said Swede.

"Not with anyone as good as I am," seriously. "If I had my way, I'd pour out every drop of liquor in this valley."

"Well," grinned Swede, "I've started in to kinda drain a village, but somebody pointed out the fact that distilleries work night shifts; so I quit."

"It is rather hopeless," sighed Aunt Ida.

"Yeah, that's right. I decided to take it by degrees."

The next day Sad rode to town with Steen, who was to post the mail and make a few purchases. Steen left Sad at the post office, which was located in a general store. They had spoken to Rios, who was just outside the post office, as they went in, and now he came in, inquiring about his mail.

Sad sat down on a counter to roll a smoke, while Rios ordered some things from the storekeeper, who was also the postmaster. Together they went in behind the little post office and into another room, but Rios came back alone, and Sad saw him halt for a moment behind the post boxes. His hand shot into the compartment of mailed letters, a quick scrutiny, and Rios came back into the store room, shoving one hand into his coat pocket.

Sad apparently paid no attention to him. Rios waited until the store keeper came back, and they talked for several minutes, before Rios left the place. Sad was sure Rios had stolen a letter, and he wondered what sort of a letter would cause a man to take such a chance.

He followed Rios over to the Singing River Saloon and saw him near the rear of the room, reading a letter. Rios put the letter in his pocket and sauntered over to a pool table, where he began knocking the balls around.

"What do yuh like to play?" asked Sad.

"I can get beat as easy at one game as another," grinned Rios.

"First eight balls in the rack makes a quick game," said Sad, and Rios racked up the balls. They removed their coats, hanging them up on hooks in the wall.

Sad accidentally knocked Rios' coat down, picked it up clumsily and hung it back on the hook. As he turned and began chalking his cue, the lone letter in Rios' coat was in Sad's hip pocket, stuffed deeply beneath his handkerchief.

Tiny Parker came in, and after Rios had beaten Sad two straight games, Sad willed his cue to Tiny and walked out. He wanted to see what was in that letter. The envelope bore an uncancelled stamp, and the name of Jim X. Smith, General Delivery, San Francisco. The enclosure read:

"DEAR JIM, — I was sure glad to get word from you. Rios just got back from Frisco and I guess he had a great time there. He was away two weeks. No real news to tell you. Things are very quiet, but a gale nearly wrecked us. There was quite a wind, but a big wind is nothing to worry about. Let me hear from you again. Sincerely,

"BILL."

Sad wrinkled his brow over this queer sort of a letter. It was stilted, artificial. What gale was Bill speaking about, he wondered? No doubt the letter was written by Bill Steen, and no one had mentioned any heavy wind in the valley.

46

"Gale?" muttered Sad. "Ga — wait a minute! Gale Reynolds. Fine."

Sad studied the letter closely, and a grin came to his lips, as he muttered, "Read the first and second line, jump every other one. Let's see what that says.

" 'Was sure glad to get word from you. Rios just got back from Frisco, he was away two weeks. No real news, but a gale nearly wrecked us. There is nothing to worry about.' "

Sad tore the letter into small bits and sifted them down through a crack in the sidewalk. He did not know who Jim X. Smith might be, but he wanted to know.

"If that was a message to someone in Frisco, they'll never git it," he decided, as the pieces sifted away.

He went back to the saloon and found that Tiny and Rios had just finished their game. Tiny invited Sad to drink with them, and as they stood at the bar, Rios apparently searched his pockets for that letter. After his drink he went back, looked along the floor and under the table.

"Lose somethin', Dell?" asked Tiny.

"It wasn't anythin'," grunted Dell. "Mebby I didn't bring it with me."

But it was evident that Rios was worried. He wandered back where he had read the letter and looked around. Then he left Tiny and Sad at the bar and went across the street, where he met Steen. Stormy See came up to them, and Steen asked him if he had seen Sontag. Before Rios could tell Steen where Sontag was, Stormy said:

"I dunno where he is now, Bill, but I seen him a short while ago settin' on the sidewalk over near the blacksmith shop, readin' a letter."

Rios blinked quickly. Sontag was seen reading a letter. He turned to Steen.

"Sontag is over in the saloon," he said. Steen crossed the street, leaving Stormy and Rios together.

"I understand that Sontag is an old friend of yours, Stormy," remarked Rios.

"Well — yeah, yuh might say he is."

"I've been wonderin' about him, Stormy. Wasn't there somethin' in the papers about a man of that name bein' mixed up in the shootin' of Dan Reynolds?"

"The paper I seen didn't mention any names."

"The name was mentioned in one paper I seen. I remember somethin' about 'em livin' in a roomin' house, but they got out next day, and managed to sneak around the police. I'm sure the name was Sontag."

"Yeah, it was," smiled Stormy. "But as soon as Reynolds was able to talk, he said they didn't do it. They was in his house, but they didn't have nothin' to do with the shootin'."

"Yeah? In his house, 'eh?"

"That's what the paper said."

"Does Steen know that?"

"Listen, Dell: I ain't runnin' nobody's business but mine. Sontag and his pardner got jobs on the Two Bar J P. How they got 'em don't make me no never mind."

"Me neither," said Rios, and walked away.

Steen found Sad at the saloon, and they rode back to the ranch. Sad tried to draw Steen out about his past life on the range, but Steen merely talked about Singing River Valley. Steen was a poor conversationalist — or didn't want to talk.

CHAPTER
FIVE

That evening the boys started a poker game in the bunk-house, but Sad didn't care to play, so he wandered out. It was bright moonlight, etching the hills and the buildings with silver. Far off in the hills a coyote chorus had started, and Sad could hear Jean playing softly on the old piano in the main room of the ranch-house.

Sad walked to a corner of the big steps, where a climbing rose had made sort of a bower, listening to Jean's playing. When she had finished, he intended going up to the door, but as he glanced past the roses he saw the figure of a man coming in from the other side.

He halted at the fence, stood there for several moments, before crawling through. The rusty barb-wires creaked, and the man crouched for a few moments, as though afraid someone might have heard the wires. Then he came cautiously to the far side of the porch. Jean was still playing, as the man went softly up the steps. Sad watched him go noiselessly to a window, peer in for a moment, and then come back to the door, where he knocked softly.

Sad had no idea who the man might be nor what his mission was; so he slipped his gun loose and stepped partly around the bush, where he could see the front door. Jean opened the door, and for several moments neither of them spoke. Then the man's voice, low and vibrant:

"Jean, I had to come. I know you hate me, and I don't blame you; but I had to come. No, don't close the door — please, Jean. You must listen to what I have to say. God knows I'm ashamed of my part in it. I came here to try and scheme how to get control of this end of the valley. I was nothing less than a sneaking spy.

"I know what they say. They say I came here to marry you, to get control of things that way. I told my father what they say and he laughed at me. He said he hoped I'd fall for you. But, Jean, as God is my judge, I didn't come to marry you. But I fell in love with you — honestly. I'm telling you the honest truth.

"But when I realized what it would mean to you — that I was seeming to try and trick you — Jean, I didn't have the nerve to tell you. You meant too much to me for that. I wasn't drunk in Singing River that night, when I told who I was. I was sick of deception — too cowardly to come and tell you the truth. I wanted to tell you more than that. I wanted to tell you that your —"

Came the crash of a revolver shot, a sharp cry from the man, and he went down with a thud. For a moment Sad was shocked to inaction. It seemed to him that the shot had been fired from the other side of the porch, and he sprang for the other side of the porch, crossing in the direct light from the open door.

There was no one in sight, and Sad went pounding around the house. The boys were running from the bunk-house, and Sad went back to join them. Jean was still in the doorway, as they crowded up the steps. In a moment Steen joined them.

The man was Gale Reynolds. Steen brought the lamp and they examined him. He was unconscious, shot through the right shoulder, bleeding quite badly.

"Came back, eh?" gritted Steen. "The poor fool. Well, we've got to get him to a doctor."

Steen stood up and looked at Jean, whose face was ashen in the lamplight.

"Where did he come from and who shot him?" he asked.

Jean blinked painfully for a moment.

"I — I don't know where he came from, Bill. He — he came to the door and started to talk with me — and somebody shot him."

"Somebody? Don't yuh know who it was?"

Sad was standing near Jean, and her eyes shifted to his face. Sad's eyes never wavered under her accusing glance.

"No," softly, "I don't know who shot him."

Steen looked sharply at Sad and back at the girl.

"Bleedin' pretty bad," said Swede. Old Lightnin' had arrived, and Sad turned to him.

"Heat me some water, Lightnin'; I sabe a little about first aid, and I can fix him up enough to git him to a doctor."

Steen started to say something, changed his mind and turned to Carey Poole. "You and Swede hitch a team to the light wagon and take off the back seat. Pile in a bunch of hay and get some blankets from the bunk-house."

Jean had plenty of nerve. She held the lamp, while Sad cut away the shirt and cleansed the wound, after which he bound it up carefully and wrapped the young man in a clean blanket. Steen, Carey Poole and Swede went to town with the injured man. Sad stood on the porch with Jean for several minutes after they drove away, and he finally said:

"Miss Proctor, why didn't yuh tell 'em that I shot the boy?"

For several moments Jean did not reply, so he said:

"Yuh feel that I did."

"I never accused you."

"You can shore talk with yore eyes, ma'am."

"I — I saw you — with a gun in your hand."

"I know yuh did. I was back of them bushes. Yuh see, I was goin' to come up and listen to yuh play the piano, but I seen this man makin' a sneak toward the house. I didn't know who he was, and I was scared it was somebody wishin' to do yuh harm, so I scroched down behind them rose bushes.

"Yeah, I heard everythin' he said to yuh, ma'am. I wasn't interested in that part of it, but I wish to gosh they'd have delayed that bullet until he told what he came here to tell. There was somethin' he wanted you to know, and the man who fired that shot didn't want him to tell it."

53

"Do you suppose that was it?" anxiously.

"Well, they shot just ahead of the confession. Here's another proof."

Sad drew out his gun and handed it to her. "I ain't had a chance to clean my gun since that shot was fired. Smell of that barrel."

But Jean shoved the gun away. "I'll take your word, Sontag, and I wish you would call me Jean. I hate Ma'am."

"Thank yuh, Jean; and my name's Sad."

"That is a queer name."

"Yeah, and I'm a queer jigger."

"Yes, I believe you are, Sad," seriously.

"Queer enough to wonder who shot Reynolds, Jean."

Jean's dark eyes looked gloomily at him. "There's no use trying to find out who shot him, Sad. Any man in this end of the valley would feel justified in doing it."

"I know — for trying to trick you."

"I wonder if he was?"

"I dunno. He sounded honest to me. Yuh know, he wanted to tell you somethin', but that bullet cut him off. He said something like, 'I wanted to tell you that your — ' Wonder what he meant?"

"I wonder. Do you think he will get well, Sad?"

"He ought to, bein' young and tough. He was bleedin' bad, but I think he could stand it. Will the doctor in Singin' River give him a even break?"

"Yes, I think he will. In fact, I know he will."

Sad went back to the bunk-house, where he sat down and tried to puzzle out who shot Gale Reynolds. It was almost a certainty that Gale came there to square himself with Jean. Was he trying to tell her something about her own men — warning her? The telegram Reynolds had received that night in San Francisco was signed Steen. Still, Bill Steen, foreman of the Two Bar J P, said he did not know Reynolds. Sad had not heard of any other Steen in that country, and the writer of that telegram was entirely too personal in that wire to not have known the man he was sending it to.

Sad could almost swear that Uncle Hewie Moore of the Bar 44 was on the square. Dell Rios was a problem — and Rios had been in San Francisco at the time Reynolds was shot. But why would Rios shoot Reynolds? Sad did not believe that the men in the taxicab were connected in any way with the cattle or sheep. He had found that Reynolds was part owner of a gambling house in San Francisco, and rather prominent in underworld politics, which would easily account for the fact that somebody wanted him at the bottom of the deep blue sea.

Was Rios connected in any way with the Reynolds interests, he wondered? Was Buck Welty put on the rim riding job to help Reynolds from that vantage point? One man could ruin everything up there.

The boys came back from town, except Steen. Swede said that young Reynolds had been pretty badly injured, but the doctor thought he would pull through. He told Sad that Steen sent a wire to Dan Reynolds.

"Didja see what he sent?" asked Sad.

"Nope, he left us down at the doctor's place."

"The whole thing is a queer deal," said Carey Poole. "The idea of that fool ever comin' back here. He should have known somebody would shoot him."

"Who do yuh think shot him?" queried Sad.

"Oh, gosh, I dunno. Plenty fellers willin' to do it."

Stormy See and Tiny Parker came out the next morning, trying to get more information about the shooting, but Sad could see that they were not very anxious to lay hands on the shooter. Stormy had another talk with Jean about Sad and Swede, advising her to keep an eye on them.

"Steen ain't exactly satisfied that they ain't friends of Reynolds," said the sheriff.

Later she questioned Bill about it, and he admitted his suspicions. He advised her to let them go, but Jean had a stubborn streak. She wanted more proof than mere suspicion.

"What was Sontag doin' near the front of the house last night?" asked Bill. "I mean, at the time young Reynolds was shot."

Jean shook her head. "I don't know, Bill."

"Did he shoot Reynolds?"

"I don't believe he did. Gale was shot in the back, and when I saw Sontag, he was on the wrong side to have done a thing like that."

Bill went away, and a little later he questioned Sad about it, but Sad seemed rather close-mouthed about the affair.

"Wasn't you close enough to hear what Reynolds told Jean?" queried Steen.

"Yeah, I heard what was said."

"Well, what was said?"

Sad smiled and shook his head. "I don't reckon Miss Proctor would thank me for repeatin' it, Steen."

"Personal, eh?"

"Well, it didn't concern any of us, if that's what yuh mean."

"Uh-huh. You didn't see the man who done the shootin', eh?"

"No, I didn't see him."

Steen seemed satisfied, and the questioning amused Sad.

Things drifted along placidly for the next few days. Gale Reynolds had a hard fight, but passed the crisis. No one was allowed to see him. Johnny Caldwell came in from the rim and reported that everything was all right. Buck Welty had not caused any more trouble. Dell Rios had been up there to see Welty, and he had assured Johnny that Welty had seen the error of his ways.

Johnny talked with Sad about the work on the rim, and Sad discovered that it was only loyalty to Jean that kept Johnny up there. He hated that kind of work.

"But I've got to be there," declared the blue-eyed, freckled-nosed cowboy. "Slim's all right, if there's somebody behind him. Tony Rush is all right, if he couldn't find any shade to set in. Nope, I've got to be up there m'self."

"How about Welty?" asked Sad curiously.

"I dunno, Sontag. Before I whipped him, he was jist plain lazy and full of hooch. Now he seems friendly — too damn friendly. He's got green eyes, and I don't like green eyes. Dell Rios came up there to have a talk with Buck, but I dunno what was said. Anyway, Dell told me that he gave Buck hell; but when Buck showed up, he didn't act as though anythin' had been said. You know dang well it ain't human nature to not show that you've been bawled out, and to hold it against the man who caused yuh to git bawled out."

"Mebbe he's scared of you, Johnny," suggested Sad.

"No, he ain't scared — he's waitin' to git even with me."

"Are you scared?"

"No, I ain't scared, but I hate to be on edge all the time."

"Did you tell Miss Proctor about it?"

"Hell — no! No-o-o-o, I wouldn't tell her."

"You ought to explain it to Slim and Tony."

Johnny laughed shortly and shook his head. "One suspicious person out of four in the same shack is enough and plenty."

"Where did Welty come from?" asked Sad.

"Panhandle country, I think. He worked for the Flyin' M outfit for a couple of years, and then he went to work for Rios. He's been with Rios almost a year."

"Must have started to work for Rios about the time Proctor was killed."

"Yeah, it was about three weeks after — I remember that now."

"Who owns the Flyin' M outfit?"

"Why, I'm not sure. I've heard it was a eastern outfit. Jim Farraday is runnin' it. The Flyin' M is quite a outfit, but I never liked the desert end of this valley, and

58

I never cared for Farraday. If he ain't a killer, he's scared. Packs a gun in a holster and one under his left armpit."

"Two-gun man, eh?"

"Yea-ah. And he's got a forked crew. They jist about take Singin' River apart when they come in. If you want to git Stormy sore, tell him yuh hear he's got a cyclone cellar, where he slides out of sight when the Flyin' M come in."

"Does he hide out?"

"Not Stormy See. He's bull-hide warp and whalebone fillin that old pelican. And Tiny is a good deputy. Nossir, them Flyin' M's shore do recognize the law of Singin' River."

The following morning the sheriff and deputy came out to the ranch. Steen, Sad, Swede and Poole were branding calves in the corral, and the two officers watched them for a while. Came a lull, as Swede and Poole cleared the corral for another bunch, and Steen and Sad went over to talk with the officers.

"Yuh ain't seen anythin' of four masked men carryin' a wounded man around here, have yuh?" queried Stormy seriously.

"What's the joke?" asked Steen.

"No joke, Bill. Las' night, about midnight, four masked men went to the doctor's house, stuck up the doctor and took young Reynolds away with 'em."

"Wasn't that a damn queer thing to do, Stormy?"

"Crazy thing to do. Hell, that kid wasn't in no shape to travel. They took everythin' off the bed along with him, and Doc. thinks they put him in some sort of a rig.

Anyway, one masked man kept a gun on Doc. for about thirty minutes, and then pulled his freight. Doc. runs all the way up to my place in his bare feet, pickin' shot out of his hide, and he —"

"Wait a minute," interrupted Tiny, his eyes full of tears. "You allus git the cart before the horse, Stormy. Yuh see, my wife's got a couple dozen chickens in a coop behind the house, and the skunks has been actin' as though she bought 'em for their benefit. Anyway, I'm up at the saloon, supportin' a poker game, and my wife thinks she hears some of her pet hens singin' a swan song; so she piles out of bed, takes my old two-barreled riot gun and goes out to salivate a polecat. She's out there lookin' around, when the Doc., dressed in a white nightgown, comes prowlin' in, tryin' to wake me up.

"Nobody answers the knock on the front door; so he goes around to the back door, jist about the time Hilda climbs over a rickety fence. She's on top of the fence, when she sees this white object glidin' around to the back door.

"Well, she lets out a yelp that means murder in Swedish, the fence busted down, and she cut loose both barrels of that shotgun. Yuh could hear it all over town, and it kinda halted the poker game. I've got me a hunch that Hilda went skunk huntin'; so I runs down to my house, and I finds her in the chicken yard, with a section of fence in her lap and agony in her voice.

"I couldn't git a word of English out of her until nine o'clock this mornin'. By golly, I've got to keep her from gettin' excited or hire me an interpreter. Now, you can go ahead, Stormy."

60

"Well," grinned Stormy, "the Doc. was so excited over losin' his patient that he didn't know he had a dozen or so shot in his anatomy, until I got down to his office. I sent one of the boys after Tiny, and then helped Doc. pick out bird-shot. He thinks one of them masked men shot him, I reckon."

"But why would they steal young Reynolds?" wondered Steen. "Did Doc. recognize any of 'em?"

"Says he didn't. They was dressed like ordinary cow-punchers, and he didn't recognize any of the voices. He said young Reynolds was too weak to care much about it."

"What do you think about it, Sontag?" asked Tiny.

"Me?" laughed Sad. "I ain't got a single idea about it, Tiny, except that it looks as though some cattlemen might have wanted to remove the son of the Sheep King. Kinda sneakin' of 'em to pick on a sick man, though."

"Might be possible," nodded the sheriff. "Still, I don't believe it. If they wanted to finish him, why be careful of him. Yuh must remember, they took bed and all — and Doc. says they really was careful of him."

"Beats me," said Steen seriously, as he coiled up his rope. "Well, we might as well mark the rest of this bunch, Sontag."

The kidnapping of Gale Reynolds gave Singing River Valley plenty of food for conversation. Uncle Hewie Moore came over to talk with Jean about it, because it had been hinted that some of the cattlemen had vented their hatred of Dan Reynolds by kidnapping his son. The old man was a little upset about it. He said he had talked with Rios, and was sure Rios had nothing to do with it.

"Well, we didn't steal him," assured Jean.

"Then that lets out this end of the valley, and it's a cinch that the outfits in the south end wouldn't have no reason for takin' him away from town."

"I don't know, Uncle Hewie," said Jean. Why did someone shoot him?"

"There yuh are? What we need is a Shylock Holmes around here."

Steen had gone to town, and came back as Uncle Hewie rode away. He came up to the front porch, his face unusually grave, and took a telegram from his pocket.

"They never seal the envelope at the depot," he told her, "and under the circumstances, I reckon — well, I read it."

He gave it to her, opened for her inspection. It read:

"Sad Sontag, Singing River, Wyo.

"Stay where you are until further orders stop paying salary and expenses. — REYNOLDS."

Jean read it quickly and looked up at Steen, who was watching her closely. She handed the telegram back to him and nervously smoothed her hair with her hands.

"Reynolds is a bigger fool than I thought," she said.

"What do you mean?"

"Planting spies in here and sending a telegram to them. Doesn't he know that he might as well write it on a postal card and send it to the post office?"

62

Steen laughed shortly. "The smarter they are the bigger mistakes they make. Anyway, this brands Sontag and Harrigan for what the are."

Jean nodded thoughtfully as she held out her hand.

"I'll give it to Sontag," she said.

"Oh, all right."

Steen gave it to her and went down to the bunk-house. Jean took the telegram, smeared some mucilage on the flap of the envelope, and sealed it. She tossed the envelope on a table in the main room, and went about her work.

CHAPTER
SIX

It was after six o'clock when the boys came in from work, and Bill Steen told Sad that there was a telegram at the house for him. Sad looked keenly at Steen, but went directly to the house, where Jean met him and gave him the telegram, without any comment. Sad hesitated about opening it, his eyes thoughtful. Finally he tore open the envelope and scanned the contents.

His lips shut tightly, as he tilted his head, one eye shut tightly, thinking swiftly. Finally he turned and handed the telegram to Jean.

"If you ain't already seen it — it might be interestin'," he said.

"I have already seen it," she replied evenly. "I sealed the envelope myself."

Sad nodded, a smile on his lips, but not in his eyes.

"That finishes me and my pardner with the Two Bar J P."

"I'm sorry," said Jean softly. "Stay to-night, won't you?"

"Did Steen see this telegram?"

"He brought it to me."

"We'll go to-night, if yuh don't mind."

"Very well, Sontag. Eat your supper and I'll have your pay made out by that time."

"Thank yuh kindly. I've enjoyed workin' for yuh."

Jean watched him leave the room, a queer expression in her eyes. If he was a spy, at least he was a gentleman and a brave man, because there was no reason why he couldn't have pocketed that telegram and said nothing about its contents.

Sad said nothing about it to anyone, until after supper, when he took Swede aside and showed him the telegram. Swede did not understand what it was all about, and he swore softly when Sad told him that they were both fired from the Two Bar J P.

"Jean Proctor and Bill Steen read this telegram before I got it," he explained to the mystified Swede. "It settled all doubts in their mind about us bein' spies for Dan Reynolds."

"But we're not," grunted Swede. "Where'd that damn shepherd get the idea that we're workin' for him?"

"Shake up yore imagination," grinned Sad. "Reynolds don't want us here, and that's the way he gets rid of us."

"Well, the dirty coyote! And after us savin' him from drownin'."

Sad laughed shortly and went to ask Carey Poole if he would take him and Swede to Singing River. Jean had no remarks to offer, as Sad drew their salaries, but there was a question in her eyes. Somehow, she could not make herself believe that Sad and Swede ever came there to do her an injury. Sad thanked her for their money.

"You are leaving the country?" she asked.

Sad smiled and shook his head. "Not unless they run us out."

"Well, good luck to you both, Sontag."

"Same to you, Miss Proctor — and a lot of it."

Swede went up to the house before they left.

"I jist had to say good-bye," he told her. "I dunno what it's all about, but Sad says it's all right; so I reckon it is."

Jean shook hands with him, and they left the Two Bar J P. Steen came up to the house as they were leaving.

"Sontag's shore got a lot of brass in his system," he told her. "Never batted an eye over this deal. A man like him never stops at anythin', and we're shore lucky to move him off this range."

"Good men with cattle, Bill?"

"As good as I ever seen — and I've seen a lot of 'em come and go."

Sad and Swede had not been back in Singing River an hour before Sad realized that Bill Steen had told others about that telegram. Stormy See was coldly cordial, and Tiny Parker seemed to try and avoid them. Swede did not notice it, not being of a sensitive nature. If people were kind to Swede he was duly grateful; if not, he did not pay any attention. Sad was different. He instinctively felt the mood of those about him, and he was able to read a man's feelings and reactions, especially if he had had any chance to observe the man under different emotions.

And Sad realized that Singing River was partly hostile toward him and Swede. At a saloon near the depot he found Jim Farraday and three of his men. Farraday was a big, burly, hard-faced cowman, partly drunk now. Sad did not know Farraday, but as Sad passed the group at the bar, a voice barked almost in his ear:

"Yo're a long ways off yore own range, ain't yuh, Sontag?"

Sad turned quickly to face a man, larger than he; a man with a long crooked nose, a scarred upper lip and a pointed chin. Sad knew him in a flash. It was Lee Welch, whom he had arrested for stealing horses in the Sundown country. Lee had proved an alibi, which Sad had never believed, but saved himself a long sentence.

"Hello, Welch," he said evenly. "You livin' here now?"

"Seem to be, don't I?" rather sarcastically.

"Ask yore friend to have a drink with us," said Farraday.

"Like hell, I will! No damn sheriff drinks with me."

Sad's eyes shifted to Farraday, and the big man was grinning in anticipation of trouble.

"Thank yuh kindly," said Sad slowly, "but I'm not drinkin'."

He turned back to Welch. "And I'm not a sheriff now, Welch."

"No-o-o-o?" Welch looked him over curiously. "Sundown got wise to herself, eh? What beats me is how in hell fellers like you ever get to be a sheriff."

"That's easy," drawled Sad, cool as ever. "They elect sheriffs like me to catch horse-thieves like you, Welch."

67

Welch snapped an unprintable epithet and grabbed for his gun, both hands down; and in that fractional part of a second it takes for a gun-man to draw and shoot, Sad's right fist hooked barely under Welch's pointed chin with every ounce of Sad's sinewy body behind it.

If Welch had been shot through the heart, he would not have fallen any quicker. The other three men yanked away from the bar, and Lentz, a tow-headed cowboy, drew his gun, but Farraday knocked it out of his hand.

"You fool," snarled Farraday. "Welch had all the best of the break; so you keep out of it, Lentz."

Lentz picked up his gun and snapped it into the holster. Sad shifted his eyes to Farraday, nodding quickly.

"Thank yuh, pardner."

"Acts like his neck was broke," offered the bartender.

"More likely his heart," said Sad. "If I remember rightly, Welch had an idea he was fast with a gun."

Farraday shifted his eyes from the unconscious Welch and looked at Sontag.

"How come yuh didn't break for yore own gun?" he asked.

"I didn't want to kill him," said Sad.

"Think yuh could?"

"Unless he can draw faster than that."

Farraday held out his hand to Sontag.

"My name's Farraday," he said. "I run the Flyin' M outfit south of here."

Sad accepted his outstretched hand and said:

"My name's Sontag."

Welch recovered enough to sit up, but he was still hazy. His eyes looked blankly around and he tried to smile. He spat painfully and got back to his feet, holding to the bar. It required a full minute after he was up to realise what had happened. The punch had driven the whisky from his brain and left a headache in its stead. He looked at Sad, and a light of understanding came into his eyes.

"I remember now," he said unsteadily. "Over in Sundown, they said you could hit like the kick of a mule. I believe it. Well, I dunno what it was all about now, but I reckon I got what I was lookin' for. Now, I'd like to buy a drink."

"I'll take a drink," smiled Sad. "I'm thirsty now."

Farraday introduced him to the other two cowboys.

"You workin' around here?" asked Bowers, a thin, wiry, swarthy faced cowboy.

"Been with the Two Bar J P."

"How's things up there?" asked Farraday.

"Fine enough."

"Girl runnin' the place, eh?" laughed Lentz.

"And runnin' it well, too. They've got all the help they can use, so me and my pardner pulled out to-day. Welch, you remember Swede Harrigan."

"Used to was yore deputy? Shore, I remember him. Is he with yuh?"

"Yeah. How are you fixed for help, Farraday?"

"Full up, Sontag. Sorry I can't use yuh."

"Oh, that's all right."

69

A little later Farraday met Stormy See. Farraday was curious about Sontag, and asked Stormy who he was.

"You've kinda got me," admitted Stormy, and told Farraday what he knew about Sad. Steen had showed Stormy that telegram, and Stormy told Farraday about it.

"And I've got a hunch that Jean Proctor fired Sontag and Harrigan on account of that telegram, 'cause it shore proves that both of 'em are workin' for Reynolds. But anybody that says anythin' worse than that about Sontag has got me to whip. I seen him pile right out in front of a bunch of steers, runnin' wild, and save a little kid's life. He may be workin' for the sheep interests, but he's a man."

Farraday had learned all he could, and a little later he met Sad and Swede in front of the post office. Sad had seen Farraday and Stormy standing in front of the sheriff's office, and he wondered if he was the subject of their conversation.

"I've been thinkin' it over, Sontag," he said. "And it kinda strikes me that I might use you two fellers. I pay fifty a month."

"All right," nodded Sad. "You'll have to furnish ridin' rigs, until we make a little money."

"That's easy enough. I'll get yuh a couple horses at the livery-stable, and we can send 'em back later."

Sad's eyes showed a certain amount of amusement, as he watched the boss of the Flying M go across the street. Then he told Swede about Welch, and their fight in the saloon.

70

"Well, what's that son of a pelican doin' here?" wondered Swede.

"Workin' for the Flyin' M. He shore grew horns for a minute, but I sawed 'em off quick. But don't go too strong on his friendship. I'd as soon trust a rattler. He made up to me right away, but he ain't the kind to take a sock on the chin and forget it. And the rest of the crew are as salty as the sea, Swede. Jist remember that Farraday packs a gun on his hip and another under his shoulder."

"Must be expectin' somethin', eh?"

"Packin' hardware thataway," grinned Sad. "Go on over and let Welch act glad to meet yuh, while I see the sheriff a minute."

Sad found Stormy at his office.

"We've quit the Proctor outfit," he told Stormy.

"I thought likely yuh would, Sontag."

"I suppose Bill Steen showed you that telegram."

Stormy's ears grew red, as he nodded his head.

"I reckon Bill spread the glad tidin's pretty thoroughly, didn't he?" asked Sad.

"We're all cattle folks up here," said the sheriff stiffly. "But what made yuh think I'd seen it?"

"Well," Sad laughed shortly, "I'd gather that much from Farraday's talk with me a while ago."

"Lot of damn old women around here," snorted Stormy. "Yuh can't tell a thing without it bein' told."

"Oh, it's all right with me, Stormy."

The sheriff got to his feet and looked keenly at Sontag. Finally he held out his hand.

"I don't give a damn who yo're workin' for," he said evenly. "I'll never forget how yuh scooped that kid away from them steers."

They shook hands solemnly, and Sad went back to join Farraday's outfit, a grin on his lips.

It is barely possible that Bill Steen wondered where Sad and Swede would go, because he came to town that day, shortly after the men had ridden away to the Flying M. He asked Stormy what became of Sontag and Harrigan, and Stormy told him that they had gone to work for the Flying M.

"I told Farraday about that telegram," said Stormy.

"And he hired 'em, eh?"

"Shore. They're a good pair of punchers, and Farraday ain't afraid of the sheep."

"I reckon that's right," agreed Steen. "They're good cowmen."

South of Singing River the character of the country changes quickly. Cottonwoods and willows gradually disappear, and the greasewood takes its place. Two miles south of the town is a semidesert, no streams, no water-holes. Creaking windmills rear their gaunt heads from the shallow cañons, working constantly for the small trickle of water, which is carefully hoarded in the man-made pools.

Thousands of acres were controlled by the Flying M. outfit. To the south of them were the Box A A, and the Lazy N Half Circle R, the latter two brands being the mark of one outfit — the Lazy N over the top of the Half Circle R. They were not big outfits, employing not more than two or three men.

The Flying M was not a pretentious group of buildings. The ranch house was a rambling old structure, weathered, badly in need of repair. The bunk-house was a long, low building, capable of housing at least thirty men. Two old windmills creaked and groaned at the main ranch, where concrete tanks held the meagre supply. The stable was a tall, sway-backed building, and there were numerous sheds and corrals.

There were no women at the ranch. Sad and Swede were introduced to Tony Zunega and Juan Garcia, a couple of Mexican horse wranglers, Doc. Bladen and Buck Terrill, two punchers, and "Welcome" Holliday, the cook.

Bladen struck Sad as being a city man, dissipated, educated far beyond the rest of them, cynical, to a point of being sarcastic. He had a broad, high forehead, greenish-gray eyes, well shaped nose and a thin-lipped mouth. In age, he could have been thirty or fifty.

Holliday was sixty, his round head covered with sparse gray hair, squint-eyed, a broken nose, which had never been set, few teeth left behind his sagging lips, and a scarred chin. If any man ever showed the scars of battle, Welcome Holliday did. Buck Terrill was small, wiry, bow-legged, with the face of a ferret, and small brown eyes, like a monkey.

Welch told Sad that Doc. Bladen did little work on the range, but spent most of his time playing cribbage with Farraday. Terrill was foreman for the Flying M, but took his orders from Farraday. Zunega and Garcia were more Yaqui than Spanish, and they spoke English with difficulty.

Neither Sad nor Swede liked the atmosphere of the Flying M. There seemed to be a strained feeling about the place. There was none of the rough bandinage of the ordinary cow outfit. Welch showed them their bunks, and let them select their ridings rigs at the saddle shed, where there was a number of fairly good saddles and bridles.

"Yuh can pick yore mounts from the remuda in the mornin'," said Welch. "We've got plenty, and a lot of 'em need ridin' out. You boys ain't particular if a horse pitches a little, are yuh?"

"No, we don't mind," said Sad. "We take 'em as they come, but we ain't goin' to appreciate anybody handin' us buckin' horses that ain't broke to handlin' cows."

"Oh, we wouldn't do that, Sontag."

"I jist mentioned that end of it," said Sad coldly, "'cause me and Swede didn't come down here to entertain an audience."

"Shore yuh didn't. I'll pick out some stuff I know is good, and you won't git anythin' we ain't already used. I'm already thinkin' about a couple cuttin' horses in that remuda that are top-notchers, but need work, and I'll see that you git 'em."

CHAPTER
SEVEN

Supper at the Flying M was rather a quiet affair. They served good food, but the conversation dragged. Sad noted that both Farraday and Doc. Bladen were half-drunk. Another thing that seemed queer was a sign on the door leading from the dining room, which said: No Admittance, Except on Business.

This was unusual at a ranch where there were no women, as the men usually had the run of the place.

"Farraday, Doc. Bladen and Buck Terrill sleep in the ranch-house," explained Welch.

"That teller Bladen seems like a queer sort to be around here," remarked Sad.

"Yeah, he shore is," agreed Welch. "Jist between me and you, I believe Doc. is a hop-head. He's from Frisco, but he's been here six months. Not a damn bit of good as a puncher, but he's smart as the devil. Farraday tells me that he's a real doctor, but his health broke down and he had to quit. Sometimes his eyes git kinda glassy, and he don't see yuh at all. I asked Farraday if Doc. wasn't a dope fiend, and Farraday told me to mind my own damn business — which answered the question pretty good."

"How did he happen to come out here?" queried Sad.

"Reynolds," confided Welch softly. "You knowed Reynolds owns this layout, don'tcha?"

"Shore, I knowed he did," lied Sad easily.

"Well, I reckon Doc. was mixed up with Reynolds in Frisco. I dunno for shore, but from what I can learn. Reynolds is mixed up in the drug business over there. Of course, this ain't to be told around — mebbe you know about it."

"I'd heard the same thing, Welch. No, Reynolds didn't tell me. He ain't the kind that tells things like that."

"No, he's pretty close-mouthed. You knowed he got shot, didn't yuh? Well, I'm bettin' it was some of that bunch he works against that got him."

"Will Reynolds come out here?" asked Sad.

"As soon as he's able to travel, I s'pose."

Sad nodded thoughtfully. "When they write to him, do they use the name of Jim X. Smith?"

"Yea-a-ah," laughed Welch. "Do you?"

"That's why I wondered if yore outfit did," smiled Sad. Swede listened blankly, marvelling that Sad knew these things. It was all rather mystifying to Swede, who was smart enough to keep his mouth shut and look wise.

A little later Welch went up to the house, where he found Bladen, Terrill and Farraday having a drink in the main room.

"Well?" queried Farraday.

"All right," nodded Welch, and helped himself to a drink. "He knows all about everythin'. Even asked me if we knew Reynolds as Jim X. Smith."

76

Farraday nodded as though satisfied. Terrill flung his cigarette in the fireplace.

"Jist the same," he said slowly, "I'd go easy with 'em, Jim, until I found out more about 'em. When Reynolds tells me they're all right, I'll trust 'em. You ain't got a thing to prove what they are."

Bladen laughed and reached for the whisky bottle.

"You're as suspicious as an old lady, Buck."

"You spend four years in the penitentiary, and you'll be suspicious yourself, Doc."

"Well," grinned Welch, "this same Sontag almost had me ticketed for a nice stretch, but I proved an alibi."

"And then tried to get even with him for it," laughed Farraday.

Welch scowled, as he helped himself to a drink.

"That ain't the end of the story," he said coldly.

"Better lay off him," grinned Terrill. "Jim told us what happened."

"I'm no damn fool," grunted Welch. "Better men than me have tried to whip him with their hands — or guns. I was half-drunk or I wouldn't have tried to throw down on him to-day; but I'm payin' for it with a sore jaw. I'm not kickin' nor provin' an alibi. He can whip me with his hands, and I'm not sayin' he couldn't draw and shoot faster than I can. But even at that, I'm not through with him."

"Well said," applauded Bladen. "You are the first horse-thief I have ever known that wasn't suffering from exaggerated ego."

"Drop that," snarled Welch.

"Drop what?" snapped Bladen.

"Callin' me a horse-thief."

Doc. straightened in his chair, his eyes boring straight at Welch.

"Cool down, you fool," growled Terrill.

"No damn hop-head can call me a horse-thief," gritted Welch.

Bladen had no gun in sight, no one saw him draw it; it was just there in his right hand, a snub-nosed automatic, going *spit! spit! spit! spit!* and Welch was caving in at the waistline, his right hand clawing up and down his holster, nerveless to grasp anything, working automatically.

Then he crashed down in a heap in a sitting position, sliding sideways on his shoulder and turning over on his face.

"God," exclaimed Terrill. "You got him, Doc."

Bladen's face was white, his lips a pencilled line, as he eyed the other two men.

"It was self-defence," said Bladen coldly. "He was reaching for his gun."

"I suppose he was," replied Farraday. "Yeah, I guess you're right. Doc."

The men in the bunk-house barely heard the four muffled reports of the automatic. Lentz got to his feet and stepped to the door.

"Was them shots?" asked Bowers.

"Sounded like it," said Lentz, "Bladen packs one of them automatics, and they don't make much noise."

Lentz stood in the doorway, watching the house, when someone came out.

"Here comes Farraday," he said, and in a moment the big man came up to the door.

"Welch and Bladen had a run-in a few minutes ago," said Farraday. "Welch reached for his gun, but Doc. beat him to it, Welch is dead."

The men crowded up to the doorway.

"Bowers," said Farraday, "you ride to Singin' River with Terrill. The sheriff and coroner have to be notified. The rest of yuh forget it. You had nothin' to do with it." He glanced sharply at Sontag. "Bladen probably saved you trouble, Sontag," he said. "Welch said he would git you for that punch yuh gave him to-day."

"My thanks to Doc. Bladen," said Sad evenly, "but I'd sooner do my own shootin'. I had nothin' against Welch. I arrested him for stealin' horses, when I was a sheriff. It wasn't anythin' personal."

"I know," nodded Farraday and went away, followed by Bowers.

The boys drifted outside, filled with curiosity, watching Bowers and Terrill saddle for their ride to town. Sad and Swede were in the deep shadows at the rear of the house, as Terrill and Bowers rode swiftly away.

"Sad, there's somethin' wrong about this place," said Swede softly. "I dunno what it is, but I don't feel right."

Sad laughed softly. "I've got a hunch it won't be so good for us, but I dunno jist what to do about it. I don't like to stick against odds like this, but — here's what I do know, Swede: Reynolds owns this place. They communicate with Reynolds under the name of Jim X. Smith, and —"

"How did you ever find that out, Sad?"

"Steen posted a letter with that name on it. Dell Rios stole the letter, read it, and I stole it from him."

Swede whistled softly. "I wondered how yuh knew so much. But this feller Steen — is he Bill Steen?"

"That's the whippoorwill. Remember that telegram on the table in Reynolds' place in San Francisco? That was from Bill Steen. He's Reynolds' man — and foreman for Jean Proctor."

"The dirty coyote! But what about Dell Rios? Ain't he got the goods on Steen?"

"That's a question. The letter sounded queer, unless yuh skipped every other line. Didn't make a lot of sense, except that it told Reynolds that everythin' was all right. I destroyed the letter."

"I'll be darned. But, Sad, what do yuh make of that telegram from Reynolds, tellin' us —"

"Probably from Reynolds. Mebbe Steen told him what to wire us. It was a scheme to disrate us at the Two Bar J P. They want us out of the country, don'tcha see it? They don't want us up there, because they've laid their plans to put sheep into that range."

"Well, wouldn't that make yuh fight yore hat! What's to be done?"

"I wish I knew. We might tell the whole story to Jean Proctor, and not be able to prove it. She suspects us. In fact, she *knows* we're employed by Reynolds, and we'd waste our breath talkin' to her. Pardner, I can already smell sheep on the north range of the Singin' River."

"That's true. I wish —"

"Sh-h-h-h-h!" warned Sad.

80

Two horsemen had turned in at the gate and were riding up to the house. At first they thought it was Bowers and Terrill coming back, but they saw that one man was riding a white horse. They rode up to the porch and dismounted. Sad and Swede slipped around the opposite side of the house and halted at the edge of the front porch, as the two men went up the steps.

Farraday heard them and flung the door open. It was Bill Steen and Jeff Ellis, foreman of the Rios outfit.

"Hello, Jim," grunted Steen.

"Hello, Bill, what brings you here to-night?"

"Plenty. Say, we met Terrill and Bowers. So Welch got his, eh? Where's Sontag?"

"Down in the bunk-house with the rest of the boys. Shut the door."

Sad took a chance, slid through the railing and dropped on his knees beside the door. It was not a good fitting front door, and he was able to distinguish nearly everything that was said. Steen was talking:

"— telegram was a fake, Jim. I had it sent, 'cause I figured to git them two away from the Two Bar J P, don'tcha see? Reynolds don't know 'em, except they was all together in a wreck and Reynolds took 'em home with him. That was the night he got shot. He says he don't know whether they shot him or not, but don't believe they did. Anyway, I sent a wire to the Cattlemen's Association to see if they knew anythin' about 'em, and here's their reply:

" 'Sontag is first-class man and has done great work for us in several rustling deals stop can not recommend him too highly.

" 'JOHN COPELY.' "

"That don't look so damn good," said Farraday.

"Good?" Bladen laughed harshly. "Remember what Welch said?"

"That's right! Welch said that Sontag knew everythin'. Knew we sent our letters to Jim X. Smith. Do you suppose somebody had the Association send him over here."

"Sure thing," grunted Bladen. "If you wasn't so damn dumb —"

"You better git yore hands on this feller right away," advised Ellis.

It was then that Sad slipped off the porch. Thirty seconds later he and Swede were mounting a dark bay and a white horse, far enough away from the house to make a safe getaway, and to still see the light from the bunk-house doorway, as one of the men, perhaps more, went into the bunk-house to summon Sad and Swede before the tribunal.

"This here comes under the headin' of horse stealin', don't it?" asked Swede, as they galloped along the road which led to Singing River.

"I'm afraid our friends back at the Flyin' M might be a little inclined to say it is, but we can't be bothered over a little thing like that."

It did not require more than a few minutes for those at the Flying M to discover that Sad and Swede were not in the bunk-house. The rest of the boys said they had not seen Sontag nor Harrigan since Terrill and Bowers had left for town.

And then Bill Steen discovered that their two horses were gone. He cursed bitterly, as did Ellis.

"They saw you come here," declared Farraday disgustedly. "Sontag is no fool. He either heard what was said, or guessed it. Now, we're in a hell of a hole. He'll go back to the Two Bar J P, tell what he knows, and you two jiggers will get a hot bullet when yuh go back."

"Why can'tcha let us have a couple fast horses?" asked Ellis. "We might catch 'em. The horses they've got are tired."

"If you were following the trail of two fools — yes," said Bladen. "Don't you suppose they'd expect you to chase 'em. Go back and brazen it out. You've got the best of 'em. Miss Proctor won't believe them."

"Mebbe not. Hell, we've got to take that chance. Nobody knows we came down here."

"Yeah, and you better go back pretty careful," advised Farraday. "You'd prob'ly meet Terrill and Bowers with the sheriff and coroner, and they might wonder where you've been."

"That's right. I reckon we better stay here until they show up, and then sneak out for home."

"Let's have a drink," suggested Bladen.

"Bring it out to the bunk-house," said Steen. "I don't like to go in there — with that *thing* on the cot."

"He can't hurt you," laughed Bladen. "Only live men can hurt you. However, if you are afraid of death, I'll bring the whisky out."

"Was it self-defence, Jim?" asked Steen, after Bladen left them.

"What's the difference?" growled Farraday. "Three of us saw it."

"I wish it had been Sontag," growled Ellis.

"Blame yourself for comin' in so openly."

"I dunno," said Steen softly. "Welch was pretty much of a mouthy fool, and he wasn't so fast with a gun. Some of us might have gone out before Sontag did."

"Some truth in that. Here comes Bladen with the liquor."

Luckily Sad and Swede saw the two men from the Flying M, the sheriff, deputy and coroner, come over the top of a rise in the moonlight, and swung off the road, until the five riders passed. They rode on to Singing River, where they dismounted on a dark side of the street, removed the bridles and tied them on the saddles. Then they turned the two tired horses loose, and went to the little hotel.

"You fellers didn't stay away long, didja?" observed the sleepy old proprietor, as he lighted their way with a lamp.

"We like yore place," grinned Sontag.

"You fellers are all right, by golly. Most everybody else kicks about the place. I heered to-night that there's been a shootin' scrape out at the Flyin' M. Feller named Welch got drilled fulla holes. Self-dee-fense, they said. Ho, ho, ho! We-e-e-ell, that's all right, too. Boys will be boys, and liars will stick together, they say. Here's yore room, and may yuh have pleasant dreams. I

84

allus feel lucky when I git to sell a four-bit room this time of night."

"We're lucky to be here," smiled Sad.

It was nearly morning when they brought Welch's body to town. Farraday, Bladen and Terrill came in with them, because the sheriff promised an early inquest, although there was no question what the verdict would be. From their hotel window Sad and Swede saw the three men from the Flying M, sauntering in and out of a saloon.

"Kinda lookin' for us," grinned Swede. "What's our move, Sad?"

"Stay where we are," replied Sad, as he polished the barrel of his Colt six-shooter with a handkerchief. "I'm not fool enough to believe in takin' big chances. Any one of them three would love to take a shot at us."

"Why don't they have us arrested for stealin' them horses?"

"And let everybody know that Steen and Ellis was down at the Flyin' M. Not a chance of that. No, pardner, we'll stay hived up a while."

Farraday found that Sad and Swede slept at the hotel, but the proprietor was unable to say whether they were in their room or not. It seemed that no one else in town knew they came back last night.

While the inquest was being held they went out, ate a breakfast, hired horses at the livery-stable and rode out of town. At the edge of town they met Dell Rios, riding alone. He looked at them curiously, nodded curtly as they passed.

"There's somethin' about that jigger I like," said Sad. "He's gaudy and good-lookin', and he may be as crooked as a dog's hind leg, but there's somethin' decent about him. Swede, I ain't a very smart gambler, but I'd almost bet a new hat that Rios was the man who shot Dan Reynolds in San Francisco."

"Where'd yuh git that notion, Sad?"

"Hunch, coupled with the fact that Rios was in San Francisco at the time of the shootin'. Jist why he should shoot Reynolds is more than I've been able to figure out."

"It's a cinch that his foreman is in with Reynolds."

"That's plenty true, or he wouldn't have been there last night with Steen. Mebbe I'll find out how close I am to the bull's-eye, if they'll let me live long enough."

"Where are we goin' now?"

"Out to the Bar 44. I may be wrong, but I've got an idea that Hewie Moore is intelligent enough to listen to reason. By this time he's heard all about that telegram, and it may be that he's gunnin' for both of us. Anyway, I'm goin' to make a showdown — if he'll listen to reason."

They found Uncle Hewie at home, and he came out on the porch as they rode up. But it was not the grinning old man they had known. He looked them over with blazing eyes and wanted to know what in hell they were doing on the Bar 44.

"We came out to have a talk with yuh, Moore," said Sad.

"Well, yuh don't! Not by a damn sight — yuh don't! I know all about both of yuh, and you better git off this

86

ranch while you've both got whole hides. Sneakin' in here, spyin' for Dan Reynolds. You git out of here and off this end of the valley, before we ornament a tree with yore dirty hides."

"You won't listen to my story, eh?" queried Sad. "Moore, I thought you had more intelligence than the rest."

Moore stepped back just inside his doorway.

"I'm jist givin' yuh time to git out of range," he said coldly. "I'm one of the best rifle shots in this danged state, I'd have yuh know."

They turned and rode away, while the old man leaned against the side of the doorway, gripping a Winchester 30-30, while Aunt Ida begged him to put down that gun and quit spitting on his vest.

"They knowed I'd massacree 'em," he told her.

"You wouldn't kill a fool hen for breakfast, Hewie. Put down that gun and act human. All they wanted to do was to talk sense with you. If they knew you as well as I do, they'd never have rode out here to try and talk sense with you."

"I'd talk sense to them with soft-nose bullets," he growled.

"Presumably. But is that a Christian way to act?"

"Christianity ain't got a thing to do with the trouble between sheep and cattle men. There's an open season on sheep and shepherds in this range, Idy. What do sheep men know about Christianity?"

"The Bible speaks of sheep and shepherds," meekly "The lamb is the symbol of meekness, Hewie. Doesn't it often mention the shepherds that watched their flocks by night?"

"Them wasn't shepherds — they was nightwatchmen. What was they watchin' 'em for at night?"

"Well," sighed Aunt Ida, "I'm sure I don't know, unless it was to keep the cowpunchers from stealin' 'em."

"Yea-a-a-ah! Well, don't preach to me, Idy. The next thing I know, you'll be askin' me to fold up m' tent and pull out, leavin' Singin' River to the shepherds."

"No, I'd never ask that, Hewie; but when two men come in all meekness, merely askin' to talk sense with you —"

"Meekness? Do you think Dan Reynolds ever hired a meek man? They can pack their talk to somebody else, and if they ever show up here — I'll meek both of 'em."

"And have their blood on your hands, Hewie?"

"No, ma'am! I'll drill 'em so far away that I won't even have blood on my land."

"Well, put away the gun, Hewie. No use standin' there, like a picture of Daniel Boone. You made your bluff."

"Bluff! If they hadn't pulled their freight, they'd 'a' been more than a bluff, y'betcha."

Uncle Hewie sighed over the fact that he had not been obliged to kill somebody, and put the gun in the corner. A sudden idea caused him to work the lever of the gun, disclosing the fact that there were no cartridges in it. He turned and looked at the complacent Aunt Ida.

"Idy," he said wailingly, "you took them shells out?"

88

"They're on the shelf over there, Hewie."

"Idy, you'll be the death of me some day."

"Mebbe, Hewie, but it won't be for murder."

CHAPTER
EIGHT

Johnny Caldwell sat in the shadow of a huge granite out-cropping, his chin in his hands, his blue eyes gazing thoughtfully down over the rolling hills. Johnny was very much in love with his boss, and that fact had caused him to day-dream very much lately. Farther back on the rim, his roan horse, reins down, cropped at the tender grass.

Johnny wanted to go back and work on the ranch, but he didn't know just how to persuade Bill Steen to take him off the rim. If he had known it, Bill Steen would have been glad to take Johnny off that job. In fact, Johnny Caldwell was one man Bill Steen wanted off the rim. But Jean Proctor realised that she could trust Johnny, and she would have blocked any movement of Steen's to take Johnny off that job.

Johnny sighed deeply, scratched his freckled nose. Suddenly a soft noise caused him to freeze statue-like. Slowly he turned his head. Just behind him, leaning across the rock, was Sad Sontag and Swede Harrigan. Johnny bit a corner of his lower lip, stared back at the valley, as though he had never seen them.

Johnny had all the latest news concerning those two, and he had let them sneak up on him. What a fine guardian he had made. No use of him trying to draw a gun. He had been a dreaming fool to allow two of Reynolds' men to capture him.

"Hello, Johnny," said Sad. Johnny slowly turned his head.

"Fingers itchin'?" queried Sad, grinning softly.

Johnny turned all the way around, careful to keep his hand away from his gun.

"I'm pretty good, don'tcha think?" he asked bitterly.

"Well, it's all accordin' who yuh ask," replied Sad. "If I was you, I'd keep more awake, Johnny. The first thing yuh know some of Reynolds' outfit will sneak up and get yuh cold."

"Meanin' yourself?" asked Johnny coldly.

Sad laughed at him and Johnny's blue eyes snapped angrily.

"Don't try to prove any alibi with me," he said.

"I'm not," said Sad quickly. "Git his gun, Swede."

Johnny shut his lips tightly, but let Swede remove the six-shooter. Sad took the gun and looked it over carefully, while Johnny eyed him wonderingly.

"Oh, it's a good gun," he said.

"Yuh don't do much target practice up here, do yuh, Johnny?"

"Naturally not."

"Yuh ain't supposed to shoot at all, eh?"

"Not unless yuh have to."

"I wondered about that."

Sad slipped the catridges from the gun and weighed them in his hand. They were the same calibre as Sad's, and he compared the weight with six from his own belt.

91

He finally loaded them in Johnny's gun, pointed the gun downward and snapped the trigger six times.

There was no more report than if the cartridges had been empty shells. Johnny's eyes opened wide, as Sad removed the cartridges again and showed him the dented primers.

"What in hell is the matter with them shells?" wondered Johnny.

"Dummy loads," said Sad. "Not even live primers. Johnny, it's a good thing yuh never *had* to shoot at somebody."

Johnny's expression of wonder changed to one of bitterness.

"That's jist like murderin' a man," he said. "Ain't there nothin' you damn sheep men won't do to a cowpuncher?"

Sad took six cartridges from his own belt, reloaded Johnny's gun and handed it back to him. Johnny took it, a queer expression in his eyes. Here he was with a loaded gun in his hand, and neither of these two men had drawn a gun. Was there a trick to it, he wondered? He licked his dry lips for a moment, took a deep breath and shoved the gun in his holster.

"That's good enough for a starter," said Sad easily, reading Johnny's thoughts. "Here's the old shells."

He handed the six dummy shells to Johnny. "It's no trick, Johnny — and we're not connected in any way with Reynolds."

Swede began rolling a cigarette, and tossed the tobacco and papers to Johnny, who started the manufacture of a smoke. His fingers shook a little.

"I'll admit I'm pretty dumb," he said. "What in hell is it all about?"

Sad rolled a smoke and sat down against the rock, hunching into a comfortable position.

"Johnny Caldwell," what would yuh say if I told yuh that Bill Steen was a Reynolds' man?"

"I'd say you was crazy, Sontag."

"Exactly — and no blame to you. Do you know Reynolds owns the Flyin' M outfit?"

"Hell, I never heard of such a thing. He's a sheep man."

"And suppose somebody told yuh that Jeff Ellis was also a Reynolds' man."

"Well," drawled Johnny, "it would make me laugh."

"And that Reynolds put Buck Welty on the rim."

Johnny scowled thoughtfully for a full minute.

"Why, damn it, Sontag, that would make Dell Rios a Reynolds' man."

"Yeah, it would. What of it?"

"It ain't reasonable. Rios owns a big outfit, and if the sheep got in here — Sontag, where didja git all them queer ideas?"

"Where did you git them dummy shells in yore gun?"

Johnny opened and closed his mouth, reached in his pocket and took out one of the dummy shells.

"They didn't even snap, did they?" he muttered. "Now, how in hell —"

"They took blank primers and reloaded shells with only the bullets," said Sad. "You'll have to check up on Slim and Tony."

"I shore will — and Welty."

"Leave Welty out of the thing, his gun is *loaded*."

"You mean to say that he shifted cartridges on us?"

"Somebody did — who else could. Yo're pretty sure of Slim and Tony."

Johnny grinned sourly. "I'm not even sure of myself now, Sontag. You've got me fightin' my hat, I tell yuh. Where'd yuh git the idea that Steen is a Reynolds' man — Steen and Ellis. Hell, you must have a — well, it ain't reasonable. Why, Steen has been foreman —" Johnny stopped and shook his head slowly. "I can't believe anythin' like that."

"Johnny, you told me that you had a big charge of dynamite, wired to shoot any old time up here on the rim. And that you had a bonfire all laid, with a five-gallon can of kerosene, ready to touch her off."

Johnny nodded quickly. "Got one of them battery boxes."

"Check up on the wirin'," advised Sontag. "And yuh might find out if it ain't water in the kerosene can."

Johnny got to his feet quickly. "What do you know about it? Did you —"

"Would I tell yuh, if I did? Don't be a fool, Caldwell. I don't know how near right I am, but if I was you I'd find out about things."

Johnny blinked rapidly and turned to look down over the valley.

"I dunno, Sontag," he said slowly. "If you're playin' some kind of a game with me, I don't sabe it. You sound honest, and yuh act honest, but I dunno. What about that telegram from Reynolds? They said yuh didn't deny anythin'. Is Reynolds payin' you two fellers?"

"No. That telegram was a scheme to drive us out. Reynolds don't want us here. Caldwell, yo're damn close to bein' sheeped out."

"Du yuh mean that, Sontag?" eyeing Sad keenly.

"Why did somebody put dummy shells in yore gun? Think hard, Johnny. The boys all know when yo're goin' down to the ranch. They know it the night before. You all take off yore guns in the evenin', don'tcha?"

"Sure."

"All right. Yo're not allowed to shoot up here on the rim, unless there is a mighty good cause for yuh to shoot. If you had fired a shot down in the valley, yore gun would have worked right, 'cause the good shells were put back, before yuh left the rim."

Johnny frowned thoughtfully, finally nodded slowly.

"It could have been done, Sontag. But how do you know it was?"

"Because yo're buckin' against brains. Reynolds will put sheep over this rim, if such a thing is possible. At least, he would, until I told yuh what I have. Look out all the time. See about that wirin' for the dynamite, and examine the kerosene."

"Yo're damn right. But what are you fellers goin' to do?"

Sad smiled slowly. "Git out or git shot, I reckon. We tried to talk sense to Hewie Moore, and he threatened to shoot us both. I can't go and talk to Jean Proctor. She wouldn't believe me on a stack of Bibles, and Steen would shoot me on sight. Jim Farraday made a mistake and thought we were workin' for Reynolds, so he hired up for the Flyin' M. Last night we escaped on horses belongin' to Steen and Ellis, and got back to town. Yuh see, Steen and Ellis came down to tell Farraday who we are. Didja know Lee Welch?"

"Yeah, I know Welch."

"Know a feller named Doc. Bladen?"

"No, I never heard of him."

"Bladen killed Welch last night in the Flyin' M ranch-house."

"The hell he did! Self-defence, I suppose."

"That's what Farraday told us."

"Well, I'll be darned. Sontag, why don'tcha have a talk with Jean Proctor? Let me go down and tell her. She'll believe me. If it comes to a showdown, I'll kill Bill Steen. Bill has always been a friend of mine, and I thought he was square as a dollar; but if he's workin' a double-cross on Jean Proctor, I'll be proud to remove him complete."

"No," smiled Sad, "I don't want anybody else to prove up on Bill."

"You choose him yourself, eh?"

"I'd like to. Yuh see, Johnny, I hate a liar."

"Shore — same here. But what about Rios?"

"The only evidence against Rios is the fact that he hired Welty to ride the rim, and that his foreman is a Reynolds' man. He might be all right. He may think Welty is all right, and he may not know that Jeff Ellis is a Reynolds' man. We better lay off Rios until we git a little more evidence."

"That's right. You say Uncle Hewie wouldn't talk to yuh?"

"Only with a Winchester rifle."

"Uh-huh. Well, the old man thinks a lot of me, and — do yuh want to stay at the Bar 44?"

"Well, it's about the only place we might stay."

"You stick here on the rim until I git back. Welty won't be back on this side until supper time, and it's doubtful if Slim or Tony will come along here. I'm goin' down and hammer some sense into the old man. Between me and Aunt Ida, I'll betcha he'll welcome yuh like a long-lost brother. *Hasta luego*."

But Johnny did not reckon with the fact that Slim Reed owned a pair of twelve-power binoculars, and that shortly after Johnny had ridden away, Slim perched himself out on a point of the rim and proceeded to investigate everything in sight.

Slim Reed was six feet three, very thin, hatchet-faced, buck-teeth, and no sense of humour. Resting the high-power glasses on a rock, he swept the edge of the rim, picked up Sad and Swede a half-mile away, but so plainly that he could almost count the buttons on their shirt.

They were humped against the rock, almost on the edge of the rim, apparently watching down the valley. Slim cased the glasses, sneaked back to his horse, and proceeded to do an Indian sneak on the two men. Slim had the latest news of them from Johnny, and there was no question in his mind that they were there for no good purpose.

So Slim played the same game on them that they had played on Johnny Caldwell, except that Slim sneaked in, threw down on them with his rifle, and collected their guns. Slim did not ask any questions. He did mention the fact that they were awful fools to ever come up on the rim.

Sad was not inclined to waste words on Slim, because Slim was not open to any sort of conviction. He forced them to mount their horses and precede him at a slow pace to their cabin, where he forced Swede to rope Sad, and afterwards Slim roped Swede, much to Swede's disgust.

"Where's Welty?" asked Sad.

"Went down to the Circle R. to-day," growled Slim. "Be back before sundown. Whatcha want him for?"

"I jist wondered where he went."

"The hell yuh did? I suppose yuh wonder where Caldwell is, eh?"

"I know where he is."

"Yea-a-ah? Where is he, Wise Man?"

"Oh, I sent him down to the Bar 44."

"*You* sent him down there?"

"Well, I didn't exactly send him, Slim, he wanted to go."

"Wait a minute, feller yo're talkin' too fast for me. Do yuh mean to say that Johnny Caldwell knows yo're up here on the rim?"

"Sure."

"Of all the liars I ever knowed, yo're the worst, Sontag. Johnny will be here by sundown, and he'll shore be surprised to hear yuh say that again."

98

Sad grinned at him, brows lifted thoughtfully.

"How long since yuh fired that six-gun of yours, Slim?"

"I dunno. Mebby a month."

"I'll betcha four-bits it won't go off."

"You'll bet me four-bits that my six-gun won't shoot?"

"Yeah."

Slim drew the gun from his holster, looked it over carefully, and glanced keenly at Sad.

"No yuh don't, feller. Suppose I fire a shot. Mebbe she's a signal, eh? Nope, I don't bite on things like that."

"Got a pair of horse-shoein' nippers around here?"

"Yeah."

"Snip the bullet out of one of yore shells. Take one out of yore gun and make the test."

Slim found the nippers and took a cartridge from his gun. It was evident that he still feared a plot of some kind. He quickly inserted a cartridge in its place, and placed the gun beside him on the table.

It was not difficult to snip through the cartridge just behind the bullet, and Slim's eyes bulged with wonder when he discovered that the cartridge contained no powder.

"Well, damn you!" he snorted at Sad. "How did yuh do that?"

"How could I do it?" smiled Sad. "I never had yore gun."

Slim's face twisted in painful concentration, as he removed the other five cartridges and clipped off the bullets. He tested a couple from his belt, and found them loaded. Then he loaded the gun again and shoved it into his holster.

"Yuh better hide them opened shells," advised Sad. "Yuh don't want anybody to know yuh found 'em."

Slim gathered them up carefully and looked curiously at Sad.

"If yuh knew they wasn't loaded, why didn't yuh throw down on me?"

"I wasn't sure about them rifle ca'tridges," smiled Sad.

Slim quickly pumped out the cartridges from the 30-30, and cut off the bullets.

"Sand enough to make 'em shake naturally!" he snorted. "Listen, feller: yo're goin' to tell me how that was done and how you knowed all about it."

"Guessed it," smiled Sad.

"Guessed, hell! Takes more'n guessin' to do a thing like that. Now, come through with the truth. I'm not goin' to —"

"Sh-h-h-h!" hissed Sad, as they heard a horse walking outside. "Don't mention it, Slim."

It was Buck Welty, half-drunk, coming back from the Circle R., where he had been to get clean clothes. Slim stepped to the doorway.

"Johnny in yet?" asked Welty.

"No."

"Good. Let's me and you have a drink, eh? Good stuff. Whoa, you damn buzzard-bait. Say! I heard that Sontag and Harrigan are back in this end of the county, and they're bein' looked for. I comes back past the Two

100

Bar J P, and Bill Steen says they're to be cracked down on at sight.

"You hadn't ort to have brought that liquor, Buck," said Slim.

"Aw, what the hell! Little liquor does yuh good. All I brought was a quart."

"C'mon in," grunted Slim. He loved liquor, but had curbed his thirst on the rim. Welty came in, carrying a sack, which contained clothes, but stopped short at sight of Sad and Swede. He blinked wonderingly, looked at Slim, who grinned in appreciation.

"Well, didja ever see such hair on a dog!" exploded Welty. "Where in hell didja git 'em, Slim?"

"Found 'em settin' on the rim a while ago."

"On the rim? Well, of all the nerve! Slim, that's worth a drink."

Welty uncorked the bottle and they both took a drink.

"How about the boys?" asked Slim.

"Not out of my bottle. Nossir, not out of my bottle. Hold yore glass."

They had another drink. The situation was so pleasant that they soon had another.

"Johnny will come back and raise hell," warned Slim, trying to refuse another drink.

"That bat-eared ranny better lay off'n me, Slim. I'm sick of him tryin' to make morals for me. From now on, he better lay off'n me. Have another drink. Slim."

"Mi's well. Here's how."

"I'll tell yuh what le's do," suggested Welty. "You lemme have these two sheep waddies, and I'll take 'em down to Circle R. I'll git Steen to come down and we'll hol' court on 'em."

"You're crazy's hell," gulped Slim. "My pris'ners, yuh unnerstan, and I'm goin' take 'em to the Two Bar J P."

"Yo're foolish. That girl gits shoft-hearted and she'll turn 'em loosh."

"Tha's what I'm goin' do jussasame. My pris'ners."

"I'll match yuh for 'em."

"You go lay a aig."

"You try make me lay a aig," belligerently. "I'll take 'em down and turn 'em over to the boys. Finish everythin' quick."

Slim braced one hand against the rough table, as he poured a stiff drink down his throat.

"Lemme tell yuh shomethin'," he said thickly, but seriously. "Them two fellers b'long t' me. You ain't got no int'res' in 'em. Keep yore hands off'n 'em, Buck."

"Yo're drunk and crazy," retorted Buck. "You stay on the rim, where yuh b'long, and I'll dishpose of 'em. I'm tellin' yuh thish, 'cause that's what I'm goin' t' do, feller."

"Thasso?" Slim stiffened quickly and his hand jerked back to his gun. "You jist try it, Welty."

"You lookin' f'r trouble?" queried Buck. "All right — you've got it!"

Both men jerked out their guns. It seemed to Sad and Swede that Welty was slow on the draw, even for a drunken man. Perhaps he did not feel the need of haste. At any rate his gun was only half out of the holster, when Slim fired.

The big revolver thundered in that small shack, and Welty, a queer expression on his face, jerked backward from the shock of the bullet, stumbled on his high-heels and crashed down against the wall, while a crimson stain appeared on his right breast. Slim clung to the table with one hand, staring white-faced at Buck. He shifted his eyes to Sad, and said soberly:

"By God, I got him!"

"Yeah, yuh got him all right, Slim," replied Sad.

"But — but he ain't dead."

"No, he ain't dead — yet. But if yuh don't git a doctor for him pretty quick, he will be dead."

CHAPTER
NINE

Slim forgot his prisoners, forgot everything, except the need of a doctor. He stumbled outside, climbed on Buck's horse, and went galloping down through the scrubby timber, heading for Singing River.

"Drunken fools," observed Sad. Slim had not roped their legs, and now Sad crossed the room to where an axe leaned against a bunk. Turning around he got the handle between his hands, worked it up until his fingers grasped the blade. Then he and Swede backed against each other, and Sad sawed Swede's bonds. Within five minutes after Slim galloped away, Sad and Swede were free, and with their guns again in their holsters.

Sad made a quick examination of Welty, and they placed him on a bunk.

"Nothin' we can do for him," said Sad. "Nothin' a doctor can do for him, by the time a doctor can git here. I reckon our best move is to get off this rim, before some more of that knot-headed bunch move in on us."

"Suits me fine," grinned Swede. "Where do we go?"

"I'm bettin' on Johnny Caldwell, so we might as well head for the Bar 44."

They took their horses from the old lean-to stable and rode back down the valley. Sad was smiling as they left the rim.

"What's so funny about it?" queried Swede.

"I was jist thinkin' what a laugh the Devil must have got out of that gun-fight."

"Laughin' at who, Sad?"

"Buck Welty. Yuh see, Buck didn't expect Slim's gun to go off."

Johnny Caldwell was out of luck. Aunt Ida met him at the ranch-house of the Bar 44, and told him that Uncle Hewie had gone to town.

"And I'm worried about him, Johnny," she said, and told how Uncle Hewie had driven Sad and Swede off the ranch.

"Now he's gone to town, where he'll meet Judge Pennington. Hewie is all swelled up over his own foolish actions, and he'll get drunk as sure as fate. I tried to persuade him to stay home, but he would go. If you see him in town, I do hope you can send him home, Johnny."

"Yes'm," rather dubiously. "Yuh see, I ain't got no right in town, Aunt Ida. I'm supposed to be guardin' the rim, but I shore wanted to have a talk with Uncle Hewie about them same men he ran away from here to-day. They're up there on the rim, waitin' for me to come back."

"Up on the rim, Johnny?"

"Yes'm, sounds funny, don't it. I — yuh see, I wanted to see if Uncle Hewie wouldn't let 'em stay here."

"Why, Johnny, they couldn't stay here — not after what folks say."

"No, ma'am, I reckon not — if yuh believe what folks say."

"Don't you?"

Johnny cuffed his sombrero down over one eye.

"No, ma'am, I don't."

"Well, goodness me! You ain't able to disprove it, are yuh, Johnny?"

"Only in my own mind."

"I'm afraid that won't be sufficient for Hewie."

"No, I reckon he'd have to have an angel come right out and tell him, before he'd believe it."

"Worse than that, Hewie don't believe in angels — not even if they had a flamin' sword."

"Well," firmly, "I'm goin' to Singin' River, Aunt Ida. It's all my job is worth — but I'm goin'."

"They can't hang yuh for doin' what yuh think is right, Johnny."

"I ain't never been hung yet," grinned Johnny.

Judge Pennington had never been a judge. In fact, he had never practised law. But he had the huge frame, equatorial rotundity, heavy jowls, red nose, beetling brows and deep bass voice usually associated with those high in the graces of the judicial gods. He affected winged collars, cut back nearly to his ears, where the gray, curling hair jutted out like horns, rusty-black, cutaway coat, worn as far back as anyone could remember him, and elastic-topped shoes, known as Congress gaiters.

A truly odd couple, he and Hewie Moore, as they stood at the bar of the Singing River Saloon that afternoon. Hewie's high-pitched voice and the rumbling bass of the Judge. For a number of years they had done their drinking together. It seemed that the Judge waited for Hewie's thirst to get the better of him, knowing that it would happen eventually, as it had to-day.

"By the gods, sir," rumbled the Judge, "I am proud of you. Hewie."

"Kinda proud of m'self," piped Hewie. "And, Judge, yuh should have seen 'em skedaddle. How them two shepherds did fade out. Bar-tender, we would have service."

"Again I repeat, I am proud of you, sir."

"I jist reached for that old thirty-thirty, pumped in a shell —" Hewie paused thoughtfully. "No, I didn't — I already had a shell in her. That was it. Will yuh slide that bottle a little, Judge?"

"With a great deal of pleasure. That is great liquor, sir. How well do I remember an occasion in which I was the guest of General Grant. Let me see-e-e. It was just before or after the — hm-m-m-m —"

"Flood?" suggested Hewie seriously.

"Flood?"

"Excuse me, Judge, I was thinkin' of Noah."

"I thought you fought with Lee," said the bartender.

"I did fight with Lee, sir. I killed Yankees until m' arm give out."

"I heard about that," said Hewie. "Wasn't it Gineral Grant that said — 'Buy Pennin'ton off and git him on our side, before he wrecks the whole damn army of ours?' "

"I did gain a certain fame," admitted the Judge.

"Yuh shore did, Judge. That's how the battle of Bull Run got its name."

"How was that?" queried the bar-tender.

"Why, they heard the Judge bellerin' for a drink before breakfast. Sho'over that bottle a little, will yuh, please; I'm drinkin' with yuh."

"Does your wife know you are here to-day?" asked the Judge.

Hewie paused in the act of pouring himself a drink.

"You do think of the most damn unpleasant things, Judge. No, she don't *know* I'm here, but she's makin' a good guess. And I'll have to set up half the night, listenin' to Scripture. The last time me and you got drunk together, she kept me awake all night, readin' Revelations. Right then, I said to her . . . 'Idy, you lemme alone after this. If I'm goin' to have snakes, let me have 'em in modified style.' To-night, me and her will prob'ly go over the dimensions of the Ark. Shove that bottle this way, will yuh? If I've got to go into the shipbuildin' business, I shore want to be all set to lay an even keel."

"By gad, sir, that is one of the reasons I have always been contented with single cussedness," rumbled the Judge.

"And the other reason is — yo're too damn ornery to live with any woman. What's the idea of allus gittin' yore arm around that bottle? Do yuh think yo're the only dry person around here?"

108

"Be moderate," begged Judge. "We have the evening before us, Hewie. "Tell me again of how you ran the shepherds off your domain."

Johnny Caldwell was in no hurry to reach Singing River. He was afraid he might meet someone from the Two Bar J P who might demand an explanation of his presence in town. It was nearly supper time when he tied his horse behind a general store, and went in through the back door.

There was Farraday and Doc. Bladen at a counter, purchasing some goods. Johnny knew Farraday, but it was the first time he had ever seen Bladen. They paid no attention to Johnny, who started toward the front of the store. Suddenly his heart gave a jerk. Here was Jean Proctor and Bill Steen coming through the front door.

Johnny ducked quickly between the ends of two counters, and got in behind a pile of blankets, which were stacked on the counter. He heard Farraday talking with Jean, and he heard Farraday introduce her to Bladen. They were talking and laughing for several minutes, while Johnny shivered for fear the storekeeper would find him there.

Finally he heard Jean telling Steen that she would be there for fifteen or twenty minutes, and he peered out to see Steen, Farraday and Bladen leave the store and go across the street. He shifted his feet and rubbed his freckled nose against the edge of a blanket.

A slight noise behind him caused him to jerk his head around. Jean Proctor was standing between the

109

ends of the two counters, looking at him. Johnny took a deep breath, straightened up and looked at her.

"I saw you come in here, Johnny," she said.

Johnny removed his hat and held it limply in both hands. His blue eyes held a deeply pained expression, while his mind went around and around, trying to think of something to put into words.

"Why did you come down here, when you are supposed to be on the rim?" asked Jean. "Is that playing fair with me?"

"No, ma'am," he managed to whisper.

"And you hid from me."

Jean brushed a lock of hair away from her cheek with a nervous gesture.

"I thought I could trust *you*," she said.

"Listen, Jean," begged Johnny, hoarsely. It was the first time he had ever called her anything but Miss Proctor.

"I — I've got a reason. Yuh see, Sontag and Harrigan —"

"What about them?"

"I — I left 'em up on the rim, and I promised —"

"You left *them* on the rim?"

"Yes,'m, yuh see, Uncle Hewie run 'em off his place, and they wanted me to fix it so they could stay there, so I came back and —"

"Johnny, have you gone entirely crazy?"

"I — I —" Johnny blinked painfully. "Yeah, I s'pose I have. Yuh see, my six-gun was loaded with dummy shells, and Sontag —"

Johnny stopped short. Bill Steen was coming in the front door. He saw them and came over, a scowl on his face.

"What are you doin' down here, Caldwell?" he demanded.

"He doesn't seem to know," said Jean wearily. "He has tried to tell me something about leaving Sontag and Harrigan on the rim — in his place, I suppose."

Johnny shut his lips tightly. He could see his finish as an employee of the Two Bar J P. Steen's eyes widened a little.

"Left Sontag and Harrigan on the rim, eh?" said Steen coldly. "Yuh didn't leave 'em up there *loose*, didja, Caldwell?"

"They wasn't tied to nothin' when I left, Steen."

"Who was with 'em?"

"Nobody."

Steen turned to Jean. "I reckon that lets *him* out, Jean."

Jean nodded and turned away. Johnny started to protest, but changed his mind and looked squarely at Steen.

"I'll take my time, Bill," he said. "It's about twenty dollars."

Steen gave him the money. "Tell me what Sontag and Harrigan are doin' up there on the rim."

"You go to hell," whispered Johnny.

"Turnin' shepherd, eh?" sneered Steen.

"You'll think so when the showdown comes, Steen."

Jean turned quickly and looked at them.

"This ain't no place to talk loud," warned Steen.

Johnny laughed recklessly. "Keep bluffin', Bill."

Steen's eyes hardened and he moved closer. Johnny's right hand was spread open just above the butt of his gun.

"There's no dummy shells in it, Bill," he said tensely.

From outside came the rattle and thud of a running horse being jerked to a quick stop, and the rider almost fell to the ground. It was Slim Reed, coming for a doctor. He yelled at someone on the street. Steen turned quickly and hurried to the doorway.

Several men crowded around Slim, who was trying to tell them to get a doctor. Steen grasped Slim by the arm, as Jean and Johnny came out, and yanked him violently.

"What happened?" he asked harshly.

"I shot Buck Welty," panted Slim. "Mebbe he's dead by now. Sontag said he would be dead if I didn't git a doctor."

"Why did you shoot Buck?" asked Steen.

"I — I dunno," blankly. "Yeah, I do know. He wanted to take my prisoners away from me."

"Yore prisoners?"

"Sontag and Harrigan. I caught 'em on the rim, Bill; so I herded 'em to the shack and tied 'em up. Welty wanted to take 'em to the Circle R, and I wanted to take 'em to the Two Bar J P."

"And so yuh got drunk and shot it out, eh?" snarled Bill. "Yeah, I can smell whisky on yuh yet."

Bill let loose of Slim and backed away from him. Jean was at the edge of the sidewalk, wondering what it was

112

all about, while Johnny stood in the doorway, grinning with the mirth he did not feel.

"So yuh captured 'em, didja, Slim?" he jeered.

Slim looked owl-eyed at Johnny.

"I shot Welty," he said foolishly. "I — I had loads in m'gun. Sontag proved that my shells were all dummies. Even the 30-30's was empty, Johnny. I cut the bullets out with the pinchers."

"What are you talking about, Slim?" asked Jean.

"He's drunk and Johnny's crazy," interrupted Bill Steen. "Here comes the doctor. Slim, you better git him a livery-stable horse; he can't drive his horse and buggy up over the rim."

"All right," said Slim nervously, and started for the stable.

Steen ran across the street, where he found Farraday, Terrill, Bladen and Ellis. Quickly he told them what had happened on the rim.

"That's our chance!" exploded Farraday. "But we've got to git there ahead of the sheriff and doctor."

They ran outside to their horses, and Bill Steen hurried over to tell Jean where they were going.

"You bring them back here," said Jean. "They are not guilty of anything — yet."

"We'll bring 'em back," replied Bill. "Where's Caldwell?"

"He ran back through the store, when you went across the street."

Muttering a curse under his breath, Bill whirled and ran back to the hitch-rack, where he mounted his horse. As they swept out of town, he rode in close to Farraday.

"Caldwell's ahead of us," he said savagely. "Somethin' has slipped, Jim, and we've got to stop Caldwell, too. By God, we'll wipe out all three of 'em, and then we'll have a clean slate."

CHAPTER
TEN

"Lis'n, Hewie," begged Judge. "Talk slower, will you? The older you get the more increas'nly hard it is to unnerstand you in moments of stress."

"Yo're drunk," declared Hewie. "Yessir, yo're drunk, Judge. Firs' time I ever drank you unner a table. Well, as far as I can unnerstand from thish babel of tongues, as the Bible would shay, Slim Reed shot Buck Welty in the cabin."

"And 'f I may be so bold as to ask, Hewie; what part of Buck's anatomy is his cabin?"

"He — he shot him on the rim, you danged old fool."

"Oh, I shee. In other words, he merely peeled him, so to speak."

"Yuh can't peel no man," explained Hewie owlishly.

"Hewie," loftily, "I am a man of fine persheptions, ver' brainy — oh, ver' brainy, you unnerstand. I know what you're talking about, but I'll be damned if I know what you mean.

"Bill Steen, Farraday, Terrill, Bladen and Ellis jist pulled out," said the bar-tender. "Slim said he had Sontag and Harrigan tied up in their cabin on the rim, and I'll bet them five jiggers are goin' up there to git 'em."

Hewie was not too drunk to realize what the bar-tender had said.

"Tha's real pity," he said solemnly. "I heartily 'prove of such proceedings, but I think thish is shomethin' worth considering. I am a hard man — oh, ver' hard. I've had to be hard. But I don' think any man should be forshibly removed from thish mundane spear, without a fair and impartial trial. Judge Pennin'ton, I shuggest that me and you mount our horshes and attend thish party."

"I have no horsh, Hewie, but no doubt a suitable mount may be shecured at the stable. It will be a pleasure, my ol' friend. Never may any man shay that Judge Pennington failed a friend in a pinch. We will take a bit of hard liquor along?"

"Neither one of you old pelicans are fit to ride a horse," said the bar-tender. "My advice is for yuh to stay here."

"Lis'n, feller," said Hewie thickly, "If anybody asks yuh if we took yore advice, yuh can pos'tively state that we didn't. C'mon, Judge."

Tony Rush, the Bar 44 cowboy, was not especially bright nor exceptionally brave. In fact, Tony was, in range parlance, a bit spooky. He would probably not hesitate to shoot a man, but horses could never drag him back to view the remains. Tony could never vouch for the old adage that dead men tell no tales, because Tony never got close enough to a dead man to find out what they might tell.

And on this day Tony came back to the cabin on the rim. It was usual that the first one back to the cabin

116

built a fire in the stove, in order to hasten the preparation of the evening meal. Tony kicked open the door, noted that he was the first one back, and decided to build a fire before stabling his horse.

He gathered up some kindling, shoved it into the old stove, poked in part of an old newspaper and touched a match. Then he sighed, straightened up, looked around and saw Buck Welty. Tony sniffed. There was a slight odour of liquor. But Tony's eyes saw the gobby stain on the breast of Buck Welty, and he froze like a pointed dog with a covey of quail under his nose.

Buck was not breathing, his sightless eyes staring at the ceiling. Buck was dead. Tony drew a whistling breath, and as though galvanized by an electric shock, whirled and went out of that cabin in two jumps. His horse whirled at Tony's sudden approach, but Tony was in the saddle in a long leap, and he whaled that horse down along the rim, beating it over the rump with his hat, riding like a maniac.

Fifteen minutes later Johnny Caldwell rode in over the rim. He saw smoke issuing from the stovepipe of the cabin; so he went carefully.

Johnny had fully made up his mind to throw his lot with Sad and Swede. He realized that Steen and his gang were not far behind him, so he made a swift entrance into the cabin, gun in hand, only to find a fire nearly burned out in the stove, Buck Welty dead, and no sign of Sad and Swede.

Johnny did not loiter in getting away from there, which was lucky for Johnny, because the five men following him had made up their minds that it was open season on Johnny Caldwell. They, in turn, made a sneak on the little cabin, and found just what Tony and Johnny had found; so, rather than incur the displeasure of the sheriff and coroner, they rode north, intending to wait and see what happened.

If Sontag and Harrigan were still on the rim, they were willing to make a try at capturing them. They were satisfied that Caldwell had beaten them to the cabin and had released the two prisoners. It was also reasonable to suppose that the three men were still on the rim.

"Damned if I wouldn't like to find out how Slim discovered them dummy shells," growled Ellis. "I'll betcha Buck thought he was goin' up against a cinch game for him."

"Sontag told him," snapped Steen. "Didn't I hear Slim tell Caldwell."

"I know that, but how did Sontag know it?"

"We'll ask Sontag," laughed Bladen. "It was your idea, wasn't it, Ellis?"

"Well, it worked until that damn Sontag showed up. If I ever git my hands on that whippoorwill, he'll tell me how he knew."

"If yuh ever do," said Terrill. "The whole damn trouble is the fact that Sontag starts thinkin' where the rest of us leave off. I wish Reynolds would git back here. We need brains on this job."

"The whole thing seems ridiculous," declared Bladen. "Welty had the rest of these rim-riders at his mercy, and all there was to do was to shove the sheep across the rim."

"That's all," growled Steen. "But when everythin' was set — Reynolds got shot. His sheep foreman wouldn't move a damn sheep without orders from Reynolds, so there yuh are. Now Welty is dead, Caldwell off the job, suspicious as the devil, and Slim Reed ready to tell the world that dummy shells had been planted in his six-gun and rifle. We're up against a tough deal right now."

The fire had died out in the stove by the time Stormy See, Tiny Parker, and Doctor Neeley, the Coroner, and Slim Reed reached the cabin. Their examination was brief. Slim swore that the body was not on the bed when he left there, and that Sontag and Harrigan were there. Stormy was disgusted with Slim's continuous gabble of things, and he proceeded to put Slim under arrest, until a coroner's jury could decide what actually happened.

"I tell yuh he was a-reachin' for his gun," protested Slim. "Why, I could prove it by Sontag and Harrigan."

"Find Sontag and Harrigan," grunted Stormy. "You had 'em tied up, didn't yuh? Well, somebody has been here since you left, and they're either headin' out of the country, or some cowman has put 'em where they can't favour sheep no more. I'm scared yore evidence ain't worth much, Slim."

"But you can't put me in jail for shootin' Buck Welty," protested Slim indignantly.

"I s'pose I can't," agreed Stormy, "but if anybody asks where yuh are, I'll have to tell 'em yo're in jail, Slim."

The sheriff balked on taking the body back with them.

"We've only got three horses, and there's four of us. I'll be danged if I'm goin' to walk."

"He'll keep here as well as in town," said Tiny, "and we can git him to-morrow."

So they drew a blanket over Welty's body, closed the cabin and went back to town. Bill Steen and his four companions were too far back on the rim to see the sheriff and his party leave the cabin. At any rate, they were not interested in the sheriff; what they wanted was a chance to catch Sad and Swede.

"They'll come back here," declared Steen. "There's no place in the valley where they can stay, so it's a cinch they'll come here to-night. If the rest of you boys want to pull back home, it's all right, but me and Ellis night-herd this cabin."

And so it was decided that Farraday, Bladen and Terrill go home. Farraday was expecting a letter or a telegram from Reynolds. Steen promised that they would bring Sad and Swede to the Flying M., as soon as they had captured them — and proceeded to hole up in a brush pile about a hundred and fifty yards from the cabin, after hiding their horses.

It was a long, tiresome wait. The sun went down, and the evening crept across the hills. They were both hungry, thirsty, but determined. It grew dark; so dark that they were unable to see the cabin.

"They won't come until later," assured Steen, when Ellis said he knew of many more comfortable places than that brush-heap.

It was about nine o'clock, and Steen was about to suggest that they go back to the Two Bar J P, have a sleep and get back early in the morning, when they saw a light in the cabin. It was sort of a pale glow through the old curtains, which hung down over the windows.

"They're back," grunted Steen. "Now we've got 'em dead to rights."

They left their brush-heap and sneaked in on the cabin. There were two saddled horses near the door but it was too dark for the men to identify them.

Cautiously they led the two animals away and tied them safely, where Sad and Swede could not find them in the dark. Then they came back and tried to see through the windows, but the windows, almost opaque from dirt, were also covered with burlap curtains.

Then, somebody blew out the light. Ellis and Steen stood close together at a corner of the shack, trying to plan out what to do. They had run their quarry to earth, but the digging out might be dangerous. Ellis wanted to leave them there until morning and take a chance on getting them when they came out, but Steen was afraid they might get away.

"You guard this window," said Steen. "I'll bluff 'em into, quittin'."

"And prob'ly git yore damn head shot off," growled Ellis.

Steen went back to the door, threw his weight against it, shaking the little cabin, and then sprang aside quickly.

"Light the lamp and open that door," he said loudly. "We've got yuh dead to rights, so yuh might as well quit."

There was no sound from within the cabin, so Steen repeated his declaration. He even found a stone and threw it against the door, making a loud clatter.

121

"Come out of there, you damn sheepherders!" he yelled. "We've got yuh cinched. C'mon out or we'll start siftin lead through the door."

Thud! Whee-e-e-e! From within the shack came the sound of a shot, and the bullet which splintered through the door barely missed Bill's head.

"So that's their game, eh?" gritted Bill. "Shove a couple bullets in through the window."

Ellis replied with a shot through the window, and ducked low, swearing viciously, when a bullet from inside the cabin splintered through the window frame and burned his left ear.

"Come out of there, you dirty sheepherders!" yelped Steen. "Come out, or we'll set fire to the cabin."

"That's the idea," said Ellis. "Let's burn the two of 'em."

Suddenly a piece of mud chinking blew out from between the logs, almost in their faces, and the bullet turned Bill's hat around on his head.

They dropped to their knees, as a high-pitched voice reached their ears:

"Who's a shepherd, dad burn yuh? Cain't a man lay down f'r a snooze without some damn drunken saddle slicker sneakin' around and callin' him names. You fool around here much longer, and they'll have to git Saint Peter out of bed to register a couple damn fools from Singin' River."

"Hewie Moore," whispered Steen.

Then came the deep rumble of Judge Pennington's voice:

122

"Hewie, have you got that bottle, sir? Damme, my two legs are bowed in the shape of a horse, and I still contend that we are lost. What is the shooting about?"

"I dunno, and what's more, you had that bottle last. Let's me and you go home, Judge — down to the Bar 44."

"And face your wife, sir? I am in no shape to listen to the Scriptures."

"Then go to sleep."

"A very pious idea, my friend. Ah, here is that bottle!"

Came the sound of a muffled *gurgle, gurgle, gurgle.*

"Here yuh are, Hewie."

Another *gurgle, gurgle, gurgle.*

"What was the shooting, Hewie?"

"Ah-h-h-h-h-h! Shootin'? Oh, yea-a-a-ah! I dunno — go to sleep."

"It awoke me, sir."

"Same here. Some drunken cowpuncher, I reckon. Didn't amount to nothin'."

When Farraday got back to Singing River he found a telegram for him from Jim X. Smith, saying that the said Jim X. Smith would arrive late that night at the Flying M. siding. Dan Reynolds usually did that. He would catch a freight train, which would let him off at the ranch siding, three miles from Singing River.

Farraday went to the ranch, and drove over from there in a buckboard. It was nearly midnight when the freight clanked in at the siding and Dan Reynolds stepped down off the caboose. He was but a shadow of the old Dan Reynolds, still half sick, crabbed.

He merely spoke to Farraday, climbed into the buckboard, and they went to the Flying M. The road was rough, which prevented much conversation, but once in the ranch house, with a bottle between them, Reynolds was anxious for news. Farraday had plenty of news, but it was mostly bad. Reynolds listened to what Farraday had to tell him, and swore bitterly.

"Why, I've got ten thousand head ready to drive," he said. "I came over here to watch them come over the rim — and you tell me this. Welty dead, the other rim-riders suspicious. What about this Sontag? Where in hell did he get all his knowledge? What is he and who is he, Jim?"

"You know as much as I do. Blame Steen. Didn't he get you to send Sontag a telegram?"

"He did. He said he wanted to drive Sontag and his partner out of the valley."

"And the fool never told me," said Farraday. "I bit on that telegram. I thought Sontag and Harrigan were your men, so I hired 'em, just like I told yuh. Welch was supposed to find out what Sontag knew. He said Sontag knew everything. Why Sontag even knew we wired or wrote you under the name of Jim X. Smith. Hell, I was sure he was yore man.

"And then Steen and Ellis, like a couple damn fools, rode down here to warn me. I suppose Sontag heard everythin' they said. Anyway, Sontag and Harrigan stole Steen and Ellis' horses and beat it for town. Bladen had a run-in with Welch, and killed him. It was self-defence."

"Always is," growled Reynolds. "But that doesn't matter. You say one of the rim-riders killed Welty, eh?"

"Slim Reed. The fool captured Sontag and Harrigan, killed Welty and headed for town. Steen, Bladen, Terrill, Ellis and myself beat the sheriff back to the cabin, expectin' to capture Sontag and Harrigan, but they was gone. Steen and Ellis are still up there, I suppose."

"Waiting for Sontag to come back, eh? He won't. The trouble with you fellows and Sontag is the fact that he's got brains. How's the kid?"

"Gettin' along all right. Bladen is a pretty good doctor. Want to see him?"

"If he's awake, yes."

They entered another room, where a lamp was turned low. Under the tumbled blankets was Gale Reynolds, pale-faced, owl-eyed. He was the reason that there was no admittance to that part of the house. Father and son looked at each other curiously.

"How are you, Gale?" asked Dan Reynolds.

"Getting along all right, I guess," coldly.

"That's fine."

Gale laughed weakly. "I suppose you are satisfied, Dad."

"Satisfied of what?"

"That one of your hired thugs knocked me out that night."

"I don't know what you are talking about."

"Dad, let's shoot square. I know it will set a precedent for you, but at least be honest with me. I came back here to square myself with Jean Proctor. Everybody, including Jean, thinks I came here to try and marry her. That's a lie, and you know it. I came here to help scheme out a way to bring sheep in here. I used an assumed name, and I fell in love with her. No, I'm not ashamed of it — the falling in love. But I was ashamed of masquerading. I stood it as long as I could, and then I — I talked too much. I was crooked; Bill Steen is crooked. She trusts Bill, and she trusted me. Go ahead and laugh. It's funny to you, Dad."

"And you almost wrecked the whole works, you fool," said his father.

"I'm sorry, Dad, but I've got a little personal pride left. But my mistake was in letting you know I was coming back here. I was honest enough to tell you I was coming to square myself. No, I'm not fool enough to think she'd ever care — again. I merely wanted her to know the truth."

"And started to tell her a lot more than your personal feelings," said Reynolds coldly.

"Which proves that you hired a man to put me out," declared the boy bitterly. "Yes, I guess I did start to tell her a few things."

Dan Reynolds shook his head slowly. "I don't understand you, Gale. I've got a fortune in sheep — a fortune that will come to you some day. And because of a touch of puppy love, you try to ruin me."

"And rather than lose your sheep — you had me shot."

Reynolds got up and paced the room several times, before he came back and stood beside the bed.

"Do you think I'd order my own son shot? I had a man watch for you. You were to be stopped — not hurt

— and brought here. But he failed to see you get off that train. He didn't expect you to drop off the rear of the train and hide in the darkness. He didn't expect you to wait an hour, sneak in and hire a livery-horse, ride out the back way and circle the town. And when he did find you — he took a chance."

"Who was that man?"

Dan Reynolds smiled thoughtfully. "What good would his name do you?"

"I want to pay him back for that shot in the dark."

"His name is Sontag."

"Sontag? The cowboy who was with you the night you were shot?"

"One of the two."

"Is he still alive?"

"I suppose he is."

"He won't be by the time I get around again."

"What makes you think that, Gale?"

"Because you gave me his name. If you wasn't through with him, you'd never have told his name. But why was I kidnapped and brought here?"

"Because you might talk. Everybody in Singing River knows who you are, and they'd love to hear what you had to say. Delirium has hung many a good man."

Gale smiled bitterly and closed his eyes.

"You go to sleep," advised his father. "Is Doc. Bladen taking good care of you?"

"That doesn't matter — I'll get along."

They went back to the main room and had another drink.

"I'd like to hear from Steen," said Farraday.

"Might be interesting. Rios never comes down here, does he?"

"No. Who will yuh send in place of Welty?"

"Who knows? Damn that rim! I've got ten thousand sheep ready to drive, and I'm feeding them hay. Get that, Jim — hay. I've got to drive. My range is all gone, and the market is rotten right now. Give me two years on this Singing River range — and sheep can go to hell, as far as I'm concerned. I'm through, after that."

"It's a bad break, Reynolds. Sontag is your Jonah."

"You just think so. I'm here now — and Jonah goes overboard."

"We've still got an edge," smiled Farraday. "Both sides are gunnin' for Sontag. The cattlemen think he's yore man, and they'd lynch him in a minute, if they could catch him."

"Well, he can't last long, not with everybody against him."

"It don't seem like he could. But Steen fired Caldwell to-day — and Sontag has told Caldwell a lot of stuff. If Caldwell starts talkin', it might be that somebody would believe him."

"Hang some crape on your ear and go to bed," advised Reynolds.

CHAPTER
ELEVEN

When Tony Rush fled from the cabin, at sight of Buck Welty's body, he was, in Tony's own words, scared stiff. In fact, he was in such a hurry that he didn't even want to be bothered with a horse. But he did, and the horse never stopped running until they came to a blank wall of granite far around at the east end of the rim.

There they stopped and Tony dismounted to let the horse catch its breath, while he calmed his shaking nerves with a cigarette.

"Gee cripes and the calves got out!" he exclaimed to himself. "Who killed Buck Welty? He's deader'n seven hundred dollars, and there ain't a soul around there. And me buildin' a fire! Whooee-e-e-e! Bronc, we shore went some. Now, who do yuh reckon gunned old Buck?"

Tony squatted on his heels and smoked his cigarette. All the kings' horses couldn't have hauled Tony back to that cabin again. Suddenly an idea assailed him. Suppose the sheriff finds that body, and suppose Johnny and Slim can both prove an alibi. What will happen to poor Tony Rush.

"I never had no trouble with Buck," wailed Tony aloud, as though someone had accused him of killing Buck. "I never —"

Tony stopped. He had forgotten the trouble between Welty and Johnny Caldwell. Perhaps Johnny had killed Buck, he thought. There was not a drop of sympathy in him for Buck Welty. Perhaps Johnny had gone to town to give himself up. Johnny would do that, reflected Tony. However, this was all guesswork. Tony settled back comfortably and decided to wait a while. It would soon be dark, and what would he do when it got dark?

"I'll jist ride down and tell Uncle Hewie," he decided. "If it comes to a showdown, I'll roll m' tarp and quit the spread. I ain't goin back to no cabin where there's been a killin' — not now nor no time."

Thus decided, he rolled another smoke. Tony knew a way down off the rim from that end, and a short-cut to the Bar 44. He was half-way down to the ranch before it got real dark, rehearsing just what he was going to say to Uncle Hewie. Tony had a wonderful speech all framed, when he rode cautiously up to the Bar 44 stable and got off his horse.

But the speech grew hazy, as he neared the ranch-house, where the lamplight spread from the curtained windows, Uncle Hewie would be hunched down on his shoulders, sock-feet on the table, reading a dog-eared book; while Aunt Ida would be on the other side of the table, mending a sock. As long as Tony had worked there, Aunt Ida had been darning a sock, and Hewie had been reading that dog-eared book.

Tony stopped at the edge of the porch. He could hear voices, and he certainly did not want to go in there and tell what he knew, if they had company. So he sneaked back and peeked in the window. There was

130

Aunt Ida in the rocker, empty hands folded in her lap, and facing her, sitting in a straight-back chair, was Sad Sontag.

Tony blinked in amazement. Sad Sontag! Tony strained his eyes, trying to see if Sad had a gun pointed at Aunt Ida. No, there did not seem to be a gun in his hand. Tony leaned back, cuffed his hat over one eye and whispered to the whole world that he'd be damned. One of Reynolds' men chatting with Aunt Ida, wife of the man who hated sheep worse than he hated anything else in the world.

"Where's Uncle Hewie?" whispered Tony. "My Gawd, mebbe he's done killed Uncle Hewie. He wouldn't never set in that house, as long as Hewie lived. Mebbe he killed Buck Welty. Sontag looked like a killer. Yessir, he's got the eyes of a killer. I better git to town and tell 'em about it."

So Tony Rush bow-legged his way down to the stable, climbed into his saddle, and headed for Singing River. No one at the ranch saw him come or go. Johnny Caldwell and Swede were in the bunk-house, letting Sad do the talking with Aunt Ida, after Johnny had told her a few truths, or his convictions, regarding Sontag and Harrigan.

Aunt Ida was open to conviction. She decided that either Sad was as honest as a dollar or the greatest single-handed liar she had ever heard.

"I suppose it's all right," she told him, "but I still don't see why, with everybody trying to kill or capture you, you still stay here."

"Jist a peculiarity, Mrs. Moore," grinned Sad.

"How do you mean?"

"I always want to leave 'em smilin', when I say good-bye."

"Well, I dunno," sighed Aunt Ida. "I do wish Hewie would come home. I'm as sure as anything that him and Judge Pennington got together this afternoon, and by this time they're —" Aunt Ida shook her head sadly. "You'll never convince Hewie," she continued.

"Never is a mighty long time, Mrs. Moore. You never could convince him that Reynolds could put sheep in over the rim, but if he don't wake up to a few facts, they'll be in here before he realises it."

"You have much faith in Reynolds, Mr. Sontag."

"Not faith — fear. He's smart, and you should always fear a smart enemy."

"Why don't you go and tell these things to Jean Proctor?"

"Because she wouldn't believe them. I don't blame her."

Aunt Ida smiled doubtingly at Sad. "The cattlemen are all against you, and still you endanger your life in staying here to try and help them. At least that is what you say. Can you wonder that they don't believe you?"

"Ain't there a parable of some kind about a feller between two mill-stones. That's me. If the cattlemen don't kill me the sheepmen will — unless —"

"Unless what?" queried Aunt Ida.

"Unless neither one of 'em do. It seems to me that me and Swede came in here and stirred up a hornet's nest. There's nothin' in it for us, no matter which way it goes."

132

Sad got to his feet and picked up his hat.

"But we're mighty poor runners, me and Swede Harrigan, ma'am. We won't run and we won't be neutral. It's askin' quite a lot of two ordinary cowpunchers to fight the sheep and cattle interests at the same time. I don't reckon we'd git far. But dog-gone 'em, they've made marked men out of us, and it's up to us to kinda zig-zag all the time. I reckon they's a order out against Johnny Caldwell by this time.

"Miss Proctor fired Johnny to-night. That hurt him a lot, Mrs. Moore. You don't know it, and I don't reckon Miss Proctor knows it, but that freckled-nose kid worships her a heap. Right now he's reckless. He'd like to ride right in and swap lead. I been talkin' with him about the cattle rustlin' that's been goin' on around here for a long time, and I'm gettin' a few ideas of my own. Nobody'd believe me — and I hate a liar worse'n I hate a snake. That's one of the reasons I'm stayin' here in Singin' River Valley — 'cause a man lied about me."

"Well," smiled Aunt Ida, "I like to hear you talk, Mr. Sontag."

"Thank yuh. I'll go out to the boys now — or would yuh like to have us go to Singin' River and find Mr. Moore?"

"No, I guess we better let him alone."

"That's sensible, Mrs. Moore. Boys will be boys, yuh know."

Tony Rush found plenty of information in Singing River. He heard that Slim Reed had killed Buck Welty

133

and that the sheriff had Slim in jail. There was much talk about Slim capturing Sontag and Harrigan, and their escape, when Slim came to get a doctor. One man told Tony that Sontag and Harrigan were the witnesses who could swear whether Slim murdered Buck or whether it was self-defence.

"But," said the man, "if somebody gets a crack at Sontag and Harrigan, they won't be any good as witnesses for or against Slim."

Tony got a few drinks and met Dell Rios to whom he explained about seeing Sontag in the Bar 44 ranch-house, talking with Mrs. Moore. Rios made no comments, and did not seem a bit excited about it. He had heard that Steen, Ellis and the men from the Flying M. had tried to capture Sad and Swede in the cabin, racing in ahead of the sheriff, but did not find them there.

"This is a good chance to capture both of 'em," said Tony.

"Yeah, if anybody wants 'em real bad," agreed Rios dryly.

Failing to excite Rios with his news, Tony had more drinks, and he was almost to the singing stage, when Steen and Ellis came back to town. They had several drinks at the bar, when Tony found them, and in his muddled way managed to tell them what he knew. They were interested. Rios saw them talking with Tony, and walked out of the place, mounted his horse and rode swiftly away into the night.

Feeling fairly secure at the Bar 44, Sad, Swede and Johnny sat up late, talking things over; and were just crawling into their blankets, when someone knocked softly on the door. Johnny went softly over to the door and said:

"Who's there?"

"Who's speakin'?" asked a voice outside.

"Caldwell," replied Johnny.

"This is Dell Rios, Johnny — alone."

"Oh!" grunted Johnny softly.

"Yuh don't need to open the door," said Rios. "I jist wanted yuh to know that a couple men are comin' right out here to try and capture Sontag and Harrigan. If yuh know where they are, tell 'em to look out."

"Thank yuh, Dell."

"Welcome. Good-night."

They heard him walk away, and Johnny went to a window, from where he saw Rios mount his horse and ride away.

"Danged queer," muttered Sad, as he pulled on his boots. "Rios warnin' us."

"Mebbe a scheme to git us outside," warned Johnny.

"My hunch is that yo're wrong. Anyway, three of us are goin' to be hard for to take."

They went outside, scattered and wandered around, meeting again at the bunk-house, where each took some blankets and went down into the willows behind the stable. Johnny and Swede got a bunch of hay, and they bedded down comfortably.

"How about layin' for them two jiggers, whoever they are?" asked Johnny.

"Mean a lot of shootin'," said Sad. "Suppose we nailed one or both of 'em — we'd have a sweet time, wouldn't we. We've got two outfits to fight now — let's keep the law neutral."

"You've got a level head," agreed Johnny.

"Level or not, it's still on top of my neck, and I'm goin' to keep it there as long as possible."

Steen and Ellis were not going to run blindly into anything. They questioned Tony about seeing Sad at the Bar 44, as the three of them rode out there together. Steen wanted to know where Harrigan was — and Johnny Caldwell — surmising that Johnny had joined them. But Tony had only seen Sontag and Mrs. Moore.

They arrived at the Bar 44, only to find the place in darkness. They sneaked in close to the house, listening at the windows, and then did the same at the bunk-house. Tony Rush was getting a bit spooky. The liquor had died within him, and he wanted a place to sleep.

"If they're in the bunk-house, they'll shoot the first man to come in there, unless he lets 'em know who he is," declared Ellis. "Sontag and Harrigan know well enough what bein' captured would mean."

Steen swore wearily, squatting on his heels against the bunk house. He was getting fed up on this sort of thing. Suddenly they heard muffled voices, the voices of two men. It was too dark to see them, but their scuffling footsteps were plainly audible. They were coming along the other side of the bunk-house.

Quickly the three men sneaked along to the front. Even in the dark, they could make out those two shadowy forms. Apparently those two men were careful not to make any more noise than necessary. One of

136

them whispered hoarsely, and they both started toward the house, coming within a few feet of the three men crouched at the corner.

It was a surprise attack, and fairly well executed. The three men hurled themselves upon the two, and for several moments there was only the sound of falling bodies, the thud of blows, hoarse grunts. Apparently the attackers did not have more than a momentary advantage, as there had been no word of victory.

One shadowy form went reeling away, caught its heel heavily and went down.

"Bite me, will yuh?" shrilled Hewie Moore's voice. "Huddem yuh, I'll show yuh!"

"Yea-a-a-a, verily!" roared the bull-like voice of Judge Pennington. "Up and at 'em, Hewie!"

"Who the hell's been down, I'd crave to ask yuh?" panted Hewie.

Came the *thud, thud, thud* of running feet, as Steen and Ellis made their getaway. The kitchen door opened, and there stood Aunt Ida, clad in a flowing night-gown, a lighted lamp in her hand, illuminating the scene. Hewie, one eye blacked, shirt half torn from his shoulders, his left hand twisted in Tony Rush's hair, stood there, legs braced apart and stared at her, while Judge Pennington, one hand across his bleeding lips, was going around and around, like a pup getting ready to lie down.

"By God, I lost my upper plate," he announced. "I had my teeth sunk in good red meat, and — and the teeth pulled out."

"I know yuh did," said Hewie dryly. "If I hadn't been tough, you'd 'a' et me up, you doggone chawer."

Tony sat down heavily, with Uncle Hewie still gripping his hair.

"Well, goodness gracious, what is it all about, Hewie?" demanded Aunt Ida. "Why are you trying to scalp Tony Rush?"

Uncle Hewie released the crestfallen, bloodyfaced Tony, who held his aching scalp in both hands.

"Found 'em," announced Judge, rubbing the sand off the plate on his knee.

"Hewie, will you tell me what was the matter?" demanded Aunt Ida. "Are you and Judge Pennington drunk again?"

"Drunk!" rumbled Judge indignantly.

"No, we ain't drunk," declared Hewie. "Me and Judge has been doin' a great and good work in the interests of the cattlemen. Of course, it never worked out right, otherwise we'd have captured Sontag and Harrigan. We were going to stay all night in the rim-rider's cabin, but Judge got to itchin' over somethin' or other, and when I lit the lamp he found a dead man in the next bunk. Nothin' must do, but we had to leave there. And when we git home, about forty damned hooligans hopped on to us. Now, you have the whole story, Idy. When Tony gits the kinks out of his vocal cords, mebbe he'll tell us somethin' interestin', eh, Tony?"

Hewie's discourse had given Tony a chance to think out a plausible lie.

138

"I was down town," said Tony painfully. "After that trouble up on the rim, I didn't want to stay up there alone, so I went to town, lookin' for you, Uncle Hewie. I didn't find yuh; so I came back jist in time to git all mixed up in a fight. I didn't know who any of the fighters was, but I jist whaled in, knowin' that right would win."

"Well, I'm sure I don't understand any of it," declared Aunt Ida. "Tony, you go to the bunk-house and go to bed. Hewie, you and Judge come in and clean up. I can smell bad liquor clear up here; and as soon as you look presentable, I shall read you a few chapters from Exodus."

"Yuh see what yuh done, Judge?" wailed Hewie. "Didn't I tell yuh she'd be layin' for us? You didn't know when we was well off."

"Well," rumbled Judge, "I'd trade a lot of chiggers and a dead man for a discourse on religion any time."

But Aunt Ida's bark was worse than her bite. She sent them to bed, after they had eaten some food, saying nothing about Sad and Swede. Johnny Caldwell met Uncle Hewie and Judge at the wash-bench the next morning, and the little old cattleman's moustache bristled at sight of the man he considered a traitor. Aunt Ida came out, all prepared to add her weight to the coming argument.

"Well, spit it out," said Hewie. "What are yuh doin' here and what do yuh want?"

"I want you to listen to a little sense, Uncle Hewie," smiled Johnny.

Hewie washed his face violently, scrubbed himself with a towel and flung it aside angrily. He looked at his wife, squinted curiously around at Johnny.

"Was you tryin' to pull all of Tony's hair out last night?" asked Johnny. "He's shore sore headed this mornin'."

Hewie scratched his head foolishly, and the Judge's laugh rumbled heartily.

"As a matter of fact, we don't know exactly what did happen," he said. "I remember that me and Hewie rode horses out of Singing River, but where we went and what we did — I don't know. And I'll bet Hewie don't know either."

"You itched, I remember that," said Hewie. "And then we found a dead man."

"Undoubtedly the body of Buck Welty," said Judge.

"Scared you plenty. Well, Caldwell, go ahead with yore talk."

"Sontag and Harrigan are down in the stable."

"What? Down in my stable? Them dad-burned sheep-herders — here?"

"Wantin' to have a talk with you," nodded Johnny.

"Sa-a-a-ay! Didn't I hoodle 'em off here with a rifle? Ain't they got no brains a-tall?"

"Calm down, Hewie," advised Aunt Ida. "I had a long talk with Sontag last night, and I'd advise you to listen to what he has to say."

"Listen? Yuh do, eh? Idy, I dunno what's wrong with you. I'll take my Winchester down there, and I'll —"

"That's right," said the Judge thoughtfully, "you are a killer. Yes, I'd advise you to go right down and kill

140

both of them. Following your natural bent for such things — you'd have to kill them."

"And after you've killed both of them — I'll make some hot-cakes," said Aunt Ida seriously.

Hewie was both mad and indignant, but he looked at his wife, and a smile twisted his thin face. He turned to Johnny, spat dryly, and said:

"All right, dad-durn yuh, I'll talk to 'em."

"Take yore rifle," advised Aunt Ida.

"You lemme alone, Idy. C'mon, Johnny."

Sad offered to shake hands with Hewie, but the old cattleman chose to ignore Sad's hand.

"Git it off yore chest," he told Sad. "I ain't had no breakfast yet."

Sad grinned at him and Hewie snorted disgustedly. Sad could see that Hewie Moore was not in a receptive mood.

"I'm goin' to tell yuh a few things, Moore," said Sad. "And no matter which way yuh see things, I'd like to have yuh take a note to the sheriff; sort of a deposition, statin' that Slim Reed shot Buck Welty in self-defence. Yuh see, Buck was one of Reynolds' men."

"Yea-a-ah? Well, that sounds interestin' — even if it ain't true. Now listen t' me, Sontag; Welty was one of Dell Rios men, and you don't think for a damn minute that —"

"I'm not askin' for any argument," interrupted Sad. "All I want to do is tell you a few things."

"I'll tell yuh one thing, Hewie," said Johnny, "every cartridge in my gun was a dummy shell. Somebody —

Welty, mebby — loaded my gun, so she wouldn't shoot."

"And he thought Slim's cartridges were the same," said Sad. "They were, until I convinced Slim, and then he loaded with good ammunition. That's why Buck wasn't so fast with his gun against Slim. He didn't know Slim had loaded shells in his gun."

Hewie's jaw sagged a little. "Why — why —" he stammered. "Lemme git this straight."

"And if I was you, I'd see about the wirin' on that dynamite signal," said Sad. "We didn't know where it was yesterday. I'll bet yuh ten to one that yore dynamite won't go off."

"Wait a minute," begged Hewie. "Yo're goin' too fast to suit me. How did you know Welty was one of Reynolds' men?"

"Guessed it."

"Oh! Yo're one of them guesser fellers, are yuh?"

"Yeah. Do you realise that you ain't got a man on the rim. Tony Rush is asleep in the bunk-house, Welty is dead, Slim in jail, Caldwell fired off the job. And you went to town last night and got drunk."

Hewie blinked painfully. He did not realise that the rim was unprotected until now.

"I'll go right over to the Two Bar J P," he said nervously. "Mebbe Jean don't realise — and I'll see Dell Rios. Gosh, we can't let this go on."

Hewie did not wait to hear any more, but bow-legged his way toward the house, where Judge was eating breakfast.

142

"I've got to git over to Rios' and Proctor's," he told Aunt Ida. "Yuh see, I jist happened to think that there ain't a man on the rim."

"What about Sontag and Harrigan?" asked Aunt Ida.

"Oh, them!" Hewie scratched his head foolishly. "They can stay here until I git back. Personally, I think they're the biggest pair of danged liars I ever come in contact with — but yuh better feed 'em, Idy. Can't even have liars starvin' to death around here. No, I ain't waitin' for breakfast."

"Hewie," said Aunt Ida seriously, "if you mention those two punchers to anybody —"

"Oh, I won't. No, ma'am, I've got more important business than that to talk about."

"You goin' to town?" asked Judge, his mouth filled with hot-cake.

"I — uh — yeah, I b'lieve I am. Sontag wants me to take a note to the sheriff."

"I'll take it in."

"Fine. Suits me. I'll see yuh later."

CHAPTER
TWELVE

"They shore had me scared," admitted Slim Reed, as he stood against the bar of the Singing River Saloon, following the inquest. "I shore never expected Sontag to send that note in, telling everybody that I gave Buck an even break. The prosecutin' attorney didn't want to pay any attention to it, but the coroner and Stormy said it satisfied them plenty."

"It was kinda funny," said Steen. "Pennin'ton wouldn't tell where Sontag was?"

"No, he wouldn't tell anythin'. I tell yuh, it was one tough night for me. But wasn't it funny about them dummy shells? If Sontag hadn't told me about 'em, Buck would have got me cold. I wonder if Buck knowed about them blank shells. That's the one thing that makes me glad I got him. Why, even them 30–30 rifle shells was all dummies."

"Are you goin' back on the rim?" asked Steen.

"I'd rather not, Bill. I'm scared I'd git the jumps up there. Is it true that you fired Johnny?"

"Yeah, he's off the ranch for good."

"Uh-huh. Well, it's shore funny about Sontag and Harrigan gittin' away, 'cause I shore had 'em tied up good. Say, I heard Tiny sayin' that Johnny had throwed in with Sontag and Harrigan. Is that right?"

"The sheepmen pay good money," said Steen meaningly.

As he turned away from the bar Hewie Moore came in.

"I been out to yore place," said Hewie. "Do you realise that we ain't got a man on the rim?"

"Where's Tony Rush?"

"Out at the ranch. Who can you send up there, Bill?"

"Might send Poole."

"I dropped in to see Dell, but he wasn't home. What's all this talk about Welty bein' a Reynolds' man?"

"Where didja hear that?" asked Steen coldly, and added quickly. "You've been listenin' to Caldwell tell what Sontag told him, eh?"

"Well, we can't be too damn careful, Bill."

"Listen to me, Hewie; would Dell Rios hire a Reynolds' man? Sontag came here to start trouble among us. Reynolds knows he can't never put his sheep in here, as long as we stick together. If he can get us fightin' among ourselves, he'll take advantage of it. That's what I told Jean. She can see it. Caldwell is a fool to play into their hands."

Hewie nodded, but there was a doubt in his mind now.

"But what about those dummy shells — the ones Sontag —"

"Reynolds is a fox," laughed Steen. "He hired brains, when he hired Sad Sontag. Jist how Sontag shifted them shells, I dunno. Anyway, he exposed his own trick to get the confidence of the boys on the rim. He never had a chance at Welty's gun. Caldwell was fool enough to fall for them."

"I — I guess yo're right, Bill. Will yuh send Poole up there? I think Tony would be willin' to go back. We'll have to see if Dell has a man. Is Slim still waitin' to hear what the coroner's jury will say?"

Slim had moved away after Hewie came in.

"They turned him loose," replied Steen. "Sontag sent a note by Pennin'ton, sayin' that Slim gave Buck an even break. Judge stayed at yore place last night, didn't he?"

Hewie nodded slowly.

"Have a drink?" asked Steen.

"Not to-day, Bill; I had mine yesterday."

"All right, I'll see about sendin' a couple men back to the rim."

A few minutes after Hewie Moore left town, Jim Farraday and a strange rider came in from the Flying M. They met Steen in front of the post office, and Farraday introduced the man as Bob Scott, from Texas. Scott was a big, hulking sort, badly in need of a shave and haircut. His small eyes were so close together that it gave him a cross-eyed look, and one jaw bulged from a huge chew of tobacco.

"Scott is an old, old friend of Dell Rios," explained Farraday, "He came to my place, lookin' for Dell — didn't yuh, Bob?"

"Yuh!" grunted Bob indifferently.

146

"Bob's such an old friend and such a damn good man that Dell will give him Welty's job on the rim."

Steen grinned knowingly. "Looks like a good man, Jim. But don't you take him out there. Sontag spilled the information that the Flyin' M. belongs to Reynolds, and, while they may not want to believe it, you better be careful. I jist had a talk with Moore, and I'm afraid Sontag and Harrigan are at his place."

"All right, you take Bob out to the Circle R. And here's orders. Set tight. Let everythin' drift along as she is now. Dan's got a scheme workin'. Leave Sontag and Harrigan alone."

"What's the idea, Jim?"

"You'll know in plenty time — but she's a dinger."

"Scott got his orders?" asked Steen.

"All he needs. You turn him over to Rios."

Uncle Hewie had talked with Jean Proctor about sending a man to the rim, but he had not mentioned the fact that Johnny Caldwell, Sontag and Harrigan were at his ranch. Jean was a little blue over the fact that she had practically fired Johnny. She had always pinned her faith in him, and after sober reflection she realised that she had not given Johnny any chance to state his side of the case.

And Johnny's retort to Steen — "There's no dummy shells in it, Bill." What did Johnny mean, she wondered? Why had Johnny dropped his hand to his gun against Bill Steen? Later Steen had explained to her that Sontag and Harrigan had probably offered Johnny more money to help them. He pointed out the fact that

Johnny was a traitor when he rode away and left Sontag and Harrigan up there on the rim. Steen was convincing, but Jean still had a doubt.

Old Lightning talked with her about it.

"I don't care what Bill Steen says," declared Lightning. "Johnny worships the ground you walk on, and he wouldn't throw yuh down."

"Don't be foolish, Lightnin'," said Jean, a trifle confused

"Aw, I'm jist a-tellin' yuh what I know. He's jist a little freckled puncher, but he's got a big heart, I'll tell yuh — and you'd be the last person he'd ever throw down. I'll admit I'm plumb s'prised at Slim. He ain't my idea of a killer. Now, if Johnny had gummed up the wheels for Welty —"

"You consider Johnny Caldwell a killer?"

"No, ma'am — not a killer, jist firm in his convictions. They're tryin' Slim to-day, ain't they?"

"Yes, I believe the inquest is to-day."

Jean walked over to the front door, as Slim rode in alone. He came up to the house, grinning from ear to ear.

"Turned loose," he told Jean. "They'd 'a' cinched me, except that Sontag sent in a note, sayin' that Welty had an even break."

"Sontag sent a note?"

Slim grinned thoughtfully. "Kinda funny, wasn't it. I been thinkin' it over on the way out. Sontag knows I'm a cow-puncher, not havin' any love whatever for sheep. And him, bein' a Reynolds' man, what do yuh suppose he got me loose for? He could 'a' kept still, and I'd

148

prob'ly be in jail for a long time. But instead of that, he goes ahead and strengthens the cowmen. Ma'am, I shore don't sabe that feller."

"Slim, what did you and Welty fight over?" asked Jean.

Slim's ears grew red, but he was honest. "Whisky — mostly. Oh, I know I was all wrong — but I drank it. Welty was already half-drunk. He wanted to take Sontag and Harrigan down to the Circle R., and I swore I'd bring 'em down here. Well, we got to arguin', and — that's how it ended."

"Slim, do yuh want to go back on the rim?" asked Jean.

"Well, I don't crave it, but I'd do it for you. Bill asked me the same thing. I wish Johnny would be back there."

"Johnny has gone over to the enemy," said Jean firmly.

"I heard that, too. Enemy?" Slim rubbed his chin thoughtfully, his eyes half closed. "I wonder," he said slowly. "Yuh see, Sontag showed me that my rifle and six-gun was loaded with dummy shells. He was all tied up at the time, ma'am. I thought he was lyin', but he was right. Then I tried to tell him that he changed 'em. But shucks, he couldn't have done it. I — I loaded my gun with good shells, before Welty showed up.

"Enemy? Dog-gone it, I can't feel thataway, ma'am. If he hadn't told me about them shells, I'd have been killed. Don'tcha see what I mean? Me with a crippled gun, buckin' against loaded shells. The sheriff examined Welty's gun, and the shells were all loaded."

"Did Welty know yore gun was crippled?" asked Lightning.

"I dunno. Buck could draw fast. I've seen him do it. And I wasn't so drunk that I didn't re'lise he drawed slow against me. If he knowed I couldn't shoot — I'm glad I got him."

"But what was Sontag doing up there on the rim — he and his partner?" asked Jean.

Slim smiled sceptically. "Said they was waitin' for Johnny Caldwell."

"Where had Johnny gone?"

"Sontag said he sent him down to the Bar 44."

"Don't it make yuh fight yore hat?" queried Lightning, as he went back to the kitchen.

"Will you saddle my blue mare, Slim?" asked Jean.

"Shore will, right away."

Steen came back to the ranch, as Jean was mounting, and after she was gone he asked Slim where she was going.

"Mebbe jist for a ride," replied Slim. "She didn't say."

"You goin' back on the rim?"

"I might," replied Slim. "Miss Proctor said she'd like to have me."

"All right. An old, old friend of Dell Rios jist showed up there, askin' for a job. Feller named Bob Scott. Dell will prob'ly send him up on the rim to take Welty's place."

"Hope he keeps sober," growled Slim, and Steen laughed.

"You can't resist temptation, eh, Slim?"

150

"I shore can — now. I don't want to kill anybody again. Why do yuh reckon Sontag got me out of jail?"

"That's easy," smiled Steen. "He's got Caldwell workin' for him, and he'll probably win you over, too."

"You mean for the sheepmen?"

"Well, he shore wouldn't help a cowman, would he?"

"No, I don't reckon. Anyway, I'm not so damn easy to lead."

"That's the stuff. If he tries any monkey business on you — go ahead and plug him plenty."

"Not if I'm sober," said Slim seriously.

Jean Proctor rode over to the Bar 44 in a troubled state of mind. She wanted to have a serious talk with Uncle Hewie, and she wanted to see if she could find out where Johnny Caldwell had gone. The latter solved itself, because Johnny was saddling a horse at the corral, as Jean rode in.

Instead of going to the house, she rode down to the corral and dismounted. It seemed to her that Johnny looked a bit grim and tired. His wide grin was missing now, as they faced each other.

"I'm glad I found you, Johnny," she said.

Johnny took a deep breath. "Thank yuh, Jean."

"I'm sorry we — I fired you that night," she said honestly

"Well," Johnny smiled wistfully at her, "I'm sorry too. But I don't blame yuh none."

"It hurt me," she said slowly. "I trusted you more than any man on the ranch, and it — it seemed as though you wasn't playing fair, when you left the rim — but there were circumstances — later."

151

"Quite a few," nodded Johnny. "But it's all right, I'm goin' back on the rim for Uncle Hewie. Yuh see," Johnny took a deep breath and smiled widely, "I'm supposed to have reformed."

"Reformed?"

"Yeah. Bad company and all that; Sontag and Harrigan."

"Oh. Where have they gone, Johnny?"

"They pulled out to Singin' River a while ago."

"Finally convinced that we didn't want them around."

Johnny shook his head slowly. "No, ma'am — fully convince that the Singin' River range *wants* to be sheeped out."

Jean weighed his words carefully.

"Then you are not exactly reformed," she said.

"Jist kinda disgusted," said Johnny. "But I'm stayin' Jean. I'll fight sheep as long as I can. Sontag and Harrigan ain't got no interests here.

"They stayed as long as they could. They didn't want me to go with 'em. Aunt Ida talked pretty harsh to Uncle Hewie, but he wouldn't listen.

"I'll tell yuh, Jean Proctor," Johnny turned and pointed at the rim, far out there in the blue haze of mid-day, "when them gray sheep come spillin' over there, like a dirty gray flood, and spew all over this end of the valley — you'll believe. But it will be too blamed late."

"Johnny, do you believe they'll really come?"

"Jist as sure as God made little apples."

152

Jean shook her head sadly. "I suppose they will, Johnny. I'm glad you are going back on the rim. Slim will go back. I'll send Bill and Lightning, if you think I should. Anyway, I'll send Carey Poole with Slim, and I'll see if Dell Rios can't send more than one. We are all short-handed. It seems funny that Reynolds hasn't sent sheep across before this, if he really had spies in here to tell him how few men we've got."

"Reynolds was shot," said Johnny, "I don't reckon his men would do anythin', except through his orders. But we've got enough men — if they would play square. I can take a dozen men and stop the sheep. They've got to come in through Badger Cañon, unless they want to travel miles over bad country. I'm shore sorry we lost Sontag and Harrigan. They're worth more than a dozen ordinary men."

"I'd like to believe that, Johnny, but all the evidence shows that they work for Reynolds."

Johnny stepped away from his horse and came over to her.

"Jean, do you know why Gale Reynolds was shot?"

"Because he was Dan Reynolds' son?"

"No, because he was goin' to tell you somethin' — goin' to expose somebody you trusted. He was kidnapped from Singin' River for fear he might recover and talk some more."

"Where is he now, Johnny?"

"I don't know where he is — whether he's alive or dead."

"How do you know these things?"

"Sontag."

"He must be close to Reynolds to know things like this. And you ask me to believe in him?"

Johnny looked at her, a queer light in his blue eyes.

"Jean," softly, "some day I'm goin' to tell yuh somethin' that yuh *ought* to believe."

"What is that?" innocently.

"Somethin'. But I'll wait until the sheep are travellin' back."

Jean turned away to hide the flush on her cheeks. But she was game.

"But suppose the sheep don't turn back," she said.

Johnny smiled wistfully. "I prob'ly won't be in no shape to ask questions."

Jean turned and held out her hand to Johnny.

"I'm glad you didn't go away with Sontag and Harrigan," she said. "Now, I'm going up and have a talk with Uncle Hewie. If we don't do something to stop cattle rustling and horse stealing, we won't have any use for the range."

"I been tellin' yuh that for a long time. Steen don't believe it, but I'll bet that a round-up will show a thirty per cent loss over the last one."

Jean nodded. "I think you are right. I talked with Stormy See, and he thinks I'm foolish. Dell Rios laughed at me."

"Uncle Hewie won't laugh, Jean; he knows."

CHAPTER
THIRTEEN

Sad and Swede were discouraged and disgusted, when they turned the horses back to the keeper of the livery-stable in Singing River.

"We've done our dangdest," sighed Swede. "For my part, I'll be darn glad to git out of this valley with a whole skin."

"We ain't out yet," reminded Sad solemnly, as they halted in front of the stable and looked up and down the street.

"We shore ain't." Swede cuffed his hat over one eye and hitched up his belt. "Let's go over and have some fun with Stormy and Tiny. At least we ain't in awful bad with the law. Here cometh Mr. Dell Rios and one tough lookin' puncher."

The tough looker happened to be Bob Scott, the old, old friend of Dell Rios, from the Panhandle. They dismounted at the Singing River Saloon and went in.

"Wouldn't anybody shoot us down in cold blood, would they?" queried Swede.

"It wouldn't be exactly ethical," smiled Sad. "Anyway, I ain't scared of Rios. He done us a good turn when he warned us out at the Box 44, so I don't reckon he's gunnin' for us."

They walked past the saloon door and stopped near the hitch-rack. Bob Scott was riding a bloodbay, wearing the Box A A brand. It was on the left side, partly hidden by the saddle tender, but Sad lifted the fender for a good look at the brand.

He stepped back, looking the animal over, and turned to see Rios and Scott in the doorway, looking at them.

"Hyah, Rios," said Swede, but Rios merely nodded coldly. Scott eyed them with evident disfavour.

"What's the idea foolin' with my saddle?" he asked coldly.

"Jist admirin' that horse," smiled Sad. "Goodlookin' animal."

"Belongs to me," stated Scott. "Saddle's mine and I own the bridle."

"Yo're quite a property owner, ain'tcha?" queried Sad.

"And I don't like nobody pawin' over m' saddle," stated Scott.

It was plainly evident that Scott was, in range vernacular, a bad boy, looking for trouble. Sad and Swede sauntered over towards them. Scott's eyes shifted sideways, but came back to them. His eyes were a peculiar slaty-gray, the whites flecked with red.

Sad stopped directly in front of him, an apologetic smile on his face.

"Yuh don't like to have anybody admire yore horse?" he asked.

"I don't want nobody pawin' at m' saddle, and don'tcha forget it."

156

"Supposin' they jist keep on pawin' at it — what then?"

"They won't keep on pawin', feller."

Sad laughed shortly. He knew quite a lot about Scott's type; the mouthy, braggart type — range rowdies.

"Where are you from?" asked Sad.

"Panhandle of Texas." He pronounced it "Takesus."

"Yuh are?" simulating great surprise. "Didja walk all the way up?"

"What do yuh mean, feller?"

"Every feller I ever met that came from the Panhandle had his horse shot out from under him by a sheriff before he ever got across the line, and had to walk north."

"Ain't no sheriff ever shot no horse out from under me!" snorted Scott belligerently.

"Yo're tough, ain'tcha?" queried Sad.

"Too tough for you, feller."

"Yeah, I'll bet you are."

Sad reached over and picked some debris from a wrinkle of Scott's shirt, while Scott gaped at him vacantly.

"Yuh ought to clean up a little," said Sad. "This ain't the Panhandle — this is civilisation."

It was too much for Scott. With a bellow of rage he struck at Sad's face, but his huge right fist struck only open air, while Sad's left fist, travelling in a short arc, collided with Scott's chin with just sufficient force to, as they say in ring parlance, knock Scott bow-legged.

157

He turned half-way around, lurching on his unsteady legs, trying to keep his balance, when Sad caught the back of his belt in both hands, started whirling him dizzily around, until Scott's feet were hardly in contact with the ground, and then threw him sprawling head over heels out into the street.

Sad leaned back against the doorway, breathing heavily. Rios was watching Scott, a smile in his eyes, while Swede was watching Rios, his right hand gripping a Colt tensed at his hip.

For several moments Scott did not move. His gun had fallen from his holster and was lying in the dust beyond him. He goggled at the three men, and got slowly to his feet. There was no fight left in Scott. He limped around in a circle, picked up his gun and slid it into his holster.

"What do yuh think of it now?" asked Sad.

"Think of what?" asked Scott.

"About bein' tough."

Scott's lips twisted queerly. "Bein' tough is all right," he said slowly, "but a feller ort to pick the right time and the right place."

Dell Rios chuckled. "I reckon we better go and buy the stuff yuh need, Scott," he said.

"All right."

As they started across the street, the sheriff came from his office with a portly looking man, dressed in a gray suit, gray felt hat. Sad and Swede saw them intercept Dell Rios, and the sheriff introduced the big man. After the introduction Stormy came on across the street, leaving Dell talking to the stranger.

158

Stormy eyed the two cowboys narrowly, as he came up to them.

"Hyah, Stormy," smiled Sad.

"Still around here, eh?"

"Yeah, we're hard to lose."

"I guess yuh are. You fellers either got a lot of luck or a lot of nerve."

"Luck," said Sad. "Who's the big feller, Stormy," pointing at the stranger with Dell Rios.

"Cattle buyer. Name's H. F. Clinton and he's buyin' for Stevens and Lane of Chicago."

"Ever done any buyin' here before?"

"Nope, this is his first trip in here. Wants anywhere from fifteen hundred to five thousand head."

Sad whistled softly. "*Some* order, Stormy!"

"Top market price, too. Take all the beef there is, and fill out with feeders."

"Most likely take all the feeders and fill out with beef," laughed Swede.

The stranger came across the street and invited them in to have a drink. Stormy introduced them to Clinton, who seemed very affable. The bartender's eyes snapped wide open at sight of the two cowboys. He had heard them cussed and discussed so much that he did not expect to see them again.

"Goin' to do some business with Rios?" asked Stormy.

Clinton nodded quickly, as he tossed off a glass of liquor.

"Yes, he thinks he can furnish about seven hundred head, possibly more."

"Yuh goin' out to the Two Bar J P this afternoon?"

"I think so. Can I make the Two Bar J P and the Bar 44 in one afternoon?"

"If yuh git started early enough."

"Are yuh in a hurry to git yore cows?" asked Sad.

"Naturally," dryly.

"Where yuh takin' yore feeders?"

"Why, I don't know yet. My job is to buy them."

"What are raw hides worth now?"

"Let's have another drink," glancing at his watch. "I've got to be on the move, boys. I wonder if I could hire one of you boys to ride with me this afternoon?"

"I don't reckon yuh could," said Sad slowly.

Stormy almost laughed, but checked himself. "I'll send my deputy with yuh, he ain't doin' anythin'."

When Jean Proctor came back from the Bar 44 she was feeling better than when she left her ranch. The talk with Johnny Caldwell, and later with Uncle Hewie and Aunt Ida had smoothed out a few things. Hewie had hired Johnny to ride the rim with Tony Rush, and intended spending part of his own time up there.

Hewie was positive that someone was stealing from him but just how it was being done he had not the slightest idea.

"I'd hire me more men, if I knowed I could trust 'em," he said. "I've got so I don't trust nobody, except m'self — and I ain't so danged sure of me."

"That there Sontag and Harrigan shore almost took us in," he told her. "By golly, they even pulled the wool over Johnny's eyes."

When Jean arrived from the ranch Bill Steen gave her the mail, and among the letters was one to Sad Sontag, the envelope bearing the imprint of Dan Reynolds, San Francisco.

Jean read the address and looked up at Bill.

"Use yore own judgment," said Bill seriously, "but I'd open it. In a time like this, yuh got to take advantage of everythin'."

She handed it to him and he opened the envelope. The enclosure read:

"DEAR SONTAG, — Your letter received. As you say, the situation is very bad. However, you have done your best, and I have no kick coming. I have changed my plans, as I feel that the risk is too great, now that things have broken against us. My advice would be to come back to San Francisco, as I have another job for you soon. Sincerely,

"REYNOLDS."

"Does that mean that Reynolds is quitting?" asked Jean anxiously.

"Shore sounds like he was," laughed Steen. "I reckon that settles any argument as to who Sontag is, Jean."

Jean drew a deep breath. "Oh, that's good news, Bill!"

"Best in the world. Might as well burn that letter, eh?"

"No, let me keep it. If Sontag ever comes back here —"

161

Steen laughed and handed her the letter, as Clinton, the cattle buyer and Tiny Parker drove in through the main gate.

Sad and Swede spent the rest of the day around Singing River. Much to Stormy See's discomfort, Sad spent quite a while in the office, perusing a copy of the brand register

"Tryin' to find some brand that ain't in it?" asked Stormy.

"I like to read 'em," smiled Sad.

"You ain't thinkin' of registerin' one, are yuh?"

"Mebbe — some day. And when I do, I'll betcha I'll have one that nobody can alter."

Stormy smiled, as he filled his old pipe. "You'd have a fine job tryin' to alter a brand like the Two Bar J P."

"Yea-a-ah? Lemme see. They brand on the right shoulder. Hm-m-m-m."

Sad got his long nose deep in the book again. Swede sauntered in and squatted against the wall.

"Tiny went away with the cow-agent, didn't he, Stormy?"

"Yeah, they went out to the Two Bar J P."

"Be back before seven o'clock, won't he?"

"Why?"

"We're pullin' out on that seven-thirty train."

"Is that right, Sontag?"

Sad looked up quickly. "Yeah, I s'pose it is, Stormy."

"Yo're wise."

"Uh-huh — I've allus figured thataway."

162

Farraday, Terrill and Doc. Bladen rode in before six o'clock, but Sad and Swede kept away from them. Farraday questioned Stormy about Sad and Swede being in town, but Stormy did not tell him that they were leaving that evening. Dell Rios and Bob Scott came back to town, and Sad saw them with Farraday and Terrill in the Singing River Saloon, after the lights were on for the evening.

Sad and Swede paid their bill at the little hotel. Tiny and the cattle buyer had not arrived, as the two cowboys walked up to the little depot. It was after seven o'clock, and the train was due at seven-thirty. Swede stopped out on the platform, while Sad went in to buy the tickets. They had decided to head for Arizona.

The depot agent was busy at the telegraph instrument, and it was several minutes before he turned to Sad, who inquired the price of their transportation.

"Was you takin' No. 6?" asked the agent.

"That's the next train, ain't it?"

"Probably will be. There's a wreck about fifteen miles down the track, and No. 6 is blocked. Freight train messed up about a quarter of a mile of track, and the Lord only knows when they'll get it cleared. You won't get a passenger out of here to-night."

As Sad turned to go out, Stormy See came in to ask about an express package. The agent told him about the wreck, and the three men talked for several minutes. When Stormy and Sad walked outside, there was no sign of Swede. Sad looked all around, wondering where Swede had gone.

"I didn't see him when I came in," said Stormy. "Mebbe he went back uptown."

"He wouldn't do that," replied Sad. "He didn't know about the wreck."

Sad called Swede's name, but there was no response. As they stepped off the depot platform, Sad stooped over and picked up a sombrero hat. It belonged to Swede. They stepped back to the light from the depot and looked it over carefully. There was no question of ownership.

"That's darned funny," mused the sheriff.

"Funny — hell!" snapped Sad. "They've jumped my pardner."

"Who has?"

"Some of yore good citizens."

"Mebbe he jist — lost the hat."

"Oh, yeah! Prob'ly laid it down to scratch his head. He *would* do that. They ganged him, I tell yuh. They're scared of me and him."

Sad took a deep breath and looked around. "The only thing that saved me was the fact that you showed up. They want us out of this country. Well, if the poor fools had only waited until a passenger train came along, they'd have been rid of us. Now, I'm goin' to deal them plenty hell, and I'll heat my own pitch."

"Keep cool," advised Stormy.

"Cool? And them with my pardner? Stormy, I was all through with this country. Me and Swede tried plenty hard to talk a language they'd understand. We're not sheepmen. We tried to save this range from sheep, but where ignorance is so damn blissful, they'll have to have sheep in order to understand that they've been doublecrossed. I'm goin' to talk in the only language these folks understand — lead language."

"Don't forgit there's a law here," warned Stormy.

Sad laughed harshly. "Go git my pardner, if yore law is worth anythin'."

"Yo're goin' off half-cock, Sontag. There's no proof that —"

"No, that's true," said Sad huskily. "Mebbe he got tired of me and ran away."

They walked down the street to the little hotel. Across the street at the Singing River Saloon, things were going full blast.

"You ain't goin' over there, are yuh?" asked Stormy nervously.

Sad shook his head. "No use, Stormy. It would only mean a killin' — and I've got plenty work to do — startin' to-morrow. I reckon I can buy me a horse and saddle at the livery-stable."

"Shore."

"Good-night."

Sad walked through the hotel, circled back to the street across from the livery-stable, and finally crossed over.

"Want to sell me that outfit I had?" he asked the keeper.

"Sell yuh the horse for fifty and the saddle for thirty. Throw in the bridle and a blanket."

"You've made a sale."

"Fine. Where's yore pardner, Sontag?"

"He's out — somewhere."

Stormy, thankful that Sontag had gone to bed, went over to the Singing River Saloon, where he met Farraday and Bladen. He told them what had happened at the depot, and his recital interested them.

"What became of Harrigan, do yuh suppose?" asked Farraday.

"I ain't got any idea, Jim. It shore looks funny."

"Sontag's on the war path, eh?"

"Y'betcha," seriously. "But he's gone to bed now. He's either a big bluff, or bad-medicine — and I'm thinkin' it's bad-medicine. He acts as though he knowed who done it — and I'm glad it wasn't me."

Bladen laughed harshly. "Somebody pulled a fast one," he said. "If they had left him alone, they'd have left town."

"Nobody knew they were goin'," said Farraday.

"I knew it," said Stormy, "but I never thought to tell anybody."

"Well, he won't git far," smiled Farraday. "Too many men lookin' for his scalp. Have a drink, Stormy."

"Shore. He denied havin' anythin' to do with Reynolds."

"Who wouldn't?" laughed Farraday, spinning a dollar on the bar. "I hear there's a buyer in here, buyin' up everythin' in sight."

"Feller named Clinton. Yeah, I reckon he'll clean out the range."

"Send him down to the Flyin' M. — I'll sell him a few. Well, here's luck."

After a few drinks Farraday and Bladen decided to go back to the Flying M. As they rode out of town Farraday remarked:

166

"I'd like to go over to that hotel and leave Sontag there for the coroner."

"Nobody stoppin' you," laughed Bladen. "I'll wait for you to do the job."

"No, thank yuh," growled Farraday. "Damn Stormy, anyway! If he'd kept away ten minutes longer, we'd have had both them trouble makers."

"Yes, and now you've only got one — the least valuable — and sent the other on the warpath."

"And jist when they was leavin' of their own accord," groaned the boss of the Flying M. "Don't tell Reynolds."

"I'll not tell him, don't worry about that. I wonder if Terrill is home yet."

It was nearly midnight when they rode in at the ranch-house. There were no lights showing. They unsaddled, fed their horses and went up to the house. Bladen lighted a lamp in the main room, and a hollow groan attracted their immediate attention.

Sprawled on the floor beside the table was Terrill, the foreman, roped tightly, bleeding a little from a scalp wound. Quickly they untied him and splashed water in his face, until he gasped, spluttered and swore.

"What's this?" grunted Bladen, picking up a sheet of paper from the table, on which was pencilled:

"FARRADAY, — When you and your trained coyotes bring Swede Harrigan back to Singing River unharmed, I'll return Dan Reynolds.

"SONTAG."

167

Bladen read it aloud, and they gaped foolishly at each other. Terrill was beginning to recover sufficiently to swear bitterly. Bladen rushed over to the room where Gale Reynolds was in bed, and found the young man propped up in bed, smoking a cigarette.

"What in hell went on out here to-night, Gale?" asked Bladen.

"All I know is what I heard," said Gale, a hint of amusement in his eyes. "I believe a Mr. Sontag herded Terrill in ahead of him, and had an interview with my father. Judging from sounds, Terrill was foolish enough to make a bad break, and the aforementioned Mr. Sontag cracked him over the head with a six-shooter.

"And then this Mr. Sontag proceeded to kidnap my father. At least, that was the gist of the conversation, and it seems that they went away after arriving at that conclusion. I believe there was mention of a note to Farraday, explaining things fully."

"Well, hell's holiday!" snorted Farraday. "That's fine business!"

"Why didn't you try to stop him?" demanded Farraday.

"Me?" Gale laughed softly and shook his head. "I've had all the bullet holes I ever need — and it might be a valuable experience for Dad."

"Yo're a hell of a son!" snapped Farraday angrily.

"Yes, and I've got a hell of a father," retorted Gale. "Go out and use up your sarcasm on Terrill. You make me laugh. I don't know this Sontag, but I heard him talk, and I'll back him against all of you. He sounds to me like a *man*."

"It's too damn bad Dan didn't wring yore neck when yuh was born."

"That's enough," said Bladen coldly. "You can't blame Gale for this. Take a little of the blame yourself, and don't be so anxious to bawl somebody else out all the time."

"Well, what's to be done?" growled Farraday.

"Fix up Terrill's head and go to sleep for a few hours. If I'm any judge, we'll not find Dan Reynolds in plain sight anywhere."

"But Sontag ain't got no place to take him."

"Don't worry about Sontag — he's well able to take care of himself. I guess he's got us over a barrel, and we'll have to make a trade."

"You fool — we can't! Harrigan knows every man in the bunch. Terrill, are yuh able to remember things?"

"Yeah, I'm all right," grunted Terrill.

"Did Harrigan know where yuh took him?"

"Of course he knows. He knows who got him, too. There was enough things said to hang the whole damn gang of us."

"A fine kettle of fish!" snorted Bladen.

"And all suckers," grinned Gale Reynolds.

"But what's to be done?" wondered Farraday. "Everythin' is all set."

"Go ahead with the deal," said Bladen. "Sontag doesn't give us any time limit. We can't let loose of Harrigan. Our best move is to go ahead, say nothing, and wait until luck breaks our way. Reynolds is as smart as a fox, and he'll whip that damn narrow-between-the-ears cowpuncher. Don't worry about Reynolds — and Sontag is no murderer."

"Rather refreshing to meet a man of that kind," said Gale. "They are scarce around this neck of the woods."

"Shut yore face, or I'll give yuh what yuh should have got before," threatened Farraday.

"All of which merely bears out my statement," said Gale dryly.

CHAPTER
FOURTEEN

It was nearly morning when Dave Fowler, the blacksmith, awoke from a deep sleep. Someone was knocking on the front door. Fowler lighted a lamp and went to the door, looking into the serious face of Sad Sontag. With him was Dan Reynolds, a stranger to Fowler.

"Well, howdy, Sontag," said Fowler, amazed, still partly asleep. "Come on in."

The two men came in, and Fowler noticed that Reynolds was carrying his hands in front of him, the wrists roped tightly. Sad looked tired and haggard, as he indicated Reynolds.

"Fowler, this is Dan Reynolds, the sheep man," he said wearily.

"Yea-a-a-ah?" Fowler drawled his astonishment.

"I'm kinda takin' care of Reynolds," said Sad. "Yuh see, Reynolds and his bunch of coyotes have been handin' me a lot of hell lately. I reckon you've heard a lot of things against me. To-night, Reynolds' men aimed to put me and my pardner, Swede Harrigan, out of the game for keeps, but they missed gettin' me.

"Anyway, they got Swede. I dunno where they took him, nor what they've done to him; so I jist went out and collected Mr. Reynolds for myself. They know I've got him, 'cause I left a note. Reynolds is my ace in the hole — my trade stuff.

"He's very, very wealthy and very smart, but I'll trade him for my pardner — even."

"And probably hang," said Reynolds angrily. "You know what the law is in kidnapping, Sontag."

"I know. But that won't interest you none."

"Why not?"

"Because yo're as guilty as I am — and I can come as near provin' my case as you can yours."

"Well, where do I come in on it?" asked Fowler.

"I came to you, because I've got to have a place to hold him for a few days, a place where they won't think to look. Fowler, I done you a favour once — remember it?"

"I shore do, Sontag. I'll never forget it."

"I want my pardner back," said Sad simply.

Fowler looked from one man to the other for several moments.

"I've got a back room," said Fowler. "It ain't got no window and only one door. Use it to store things, but I can move in an old bed."

"You'll regret this," said Reynolds coldly.

"Yeah, I reckon," said Fowler. "But I allus like to pay my debts."

Terrill, his head well bandaged, came to Singing River the next day with Doc. Bladen. Terrill was very bitter over what Sontag had done to him, and he had told Bladen what he was going to do to Sontag. But when he met Sontag on the street, a Sontag who looked critically at the bandaged head and nodded his approval, Terrill lost his nerve.

"We got your note, Sontag," said Doc. Bladen.

"That's fine — and yuh can believe every word of it."

"You've got a lot of nerve — stayin' around here," growled Terrill.

"I'm jist waitin' for yuh to bring my pardner back."

"Damn yuh, we ain't got him."

Sad shrugged his shoulders. "That don't interest me, Terrill. I've got some tradin' stock, any time yo're ready to do business. And another thing to remember: I've got Reynolds where the hair is short. If anythin' happens to me — Reynolds gits his. And whatever happens to Swede Harrigan — Reynolds gits the same medicine."

"You're bucking a tough game," said Bladen.

"Not so tough," said Sad seriously. "Plenty bloodthirsty, but lackin' brains. Yuh see, me and Swede was leavin' town last night, but you and yore brainless crew stopped the deal."

"Yo're not leavin' now, eh?" queried Terrill.

"Not so yuh could notice it. I've got yore brains roped."

Bladen laughed, as they went on. Sad met Tiny Parker, and Tiny was full of questions about Swede. Stormy had told Tiny about the disappearance of Swede.

"Yeah, they got him," said Sad.

"Who — the cattlemen?"

"I hope not," smiled Sad.

Tiny told of going to the Two Bar J P and the Bar 44 with Clinton, the buyer.

"Knows about as much about cows as I do about reindeer," said the fat deputy. "But he shore buys plentiful. He'll jist about clean up this range in a hurry. Wants 'em to round-up everythin' and throw 'em on that big flat, this side of the Bar 44."

"Price right?" asked Sad.

"Y'betcha. He won't argue. Says he wants plenty cows and he wants 'em right away. And every ranch is short of help for a round-up. I'll bet even *you* could git a job now."

"They must be awful short of help," smiled Sad, and went over to the sheriff's office, where Stormy glared at him.

"Find yore pardner?"

"No — not yet."

"Huh!" Stormy bristled a little. "Bill Steen was in this mornin'. It seems that Dan Reynolds wrote you a letter."

"Did he?"

"Yea-a-ah. Sent it to you in care of the Two Bar J P."

"And Steen opened it."

"Well, what can yuh expect? It had Reynolds' name on the envelope."

Sad grinned thoughtfully. "That was thoughtful of him."

"Yeah. It said for you to come back to Frisco and go to work on another job, 'cause he was droppin' the idea of puttin' sheep in this range. My advice to you,

174

Sontag, would be to git to hell out of here, before the boys decorate a tree with yuh."

"You ain't tryin' to scare me, are yuh, Stormy?"

"I'm jist givin' yuh some good advice."

"Thank yuh, but I'm all filled up," said Sad, and walked out of the office.

Sad was not afraid for his own skin now — not from the sheepmen. They would handle him with kid gloves, until they had Reynolds. Sad got his horse and rode out to the Two Bar J P. Jean was there alone, except for old Lightning, the cook, and her eyes were uncompromising, when she looked at Sad.

"I didn't come out here askin' for any mercy," he told her smiling. "Stormy told me about that letter, and I'd jist kinda like to look at the envelope."

"I don't know why I should show it to you," said Jean evenly.

"I don't either, except that I'd like to see it. It can't do any harm."

After due deliberation Jean showed him the empty envelope, and he examined it closely. Finally he looked up at her, a smile on his lips.

"Not a bad piece of work," he told her. "Won't stand close inspection, of course — but not bad. Take a close look at that San Francisco postmark and the one at Singin' River. Yuh might also look at the cancellation on the stamp. Notice them black lines on the stamp, and yuh can see they don't fit the same lines on the envelope. Ma'am, that there letter never even seen the inside of a post office."

Jean frowned over the envelope for a long time, and when she looked up, there was a queer expression in her eyes.

"Why, it looks as though it had been done by hand," she said.

"The whole thing's faked, Miss Proctor. That letter couldn't have come from Dan Reynolds in San Francisco, 'cause I've got Dan Reynolds all tied up and under lock and key."

"You've what!"

"Yes'm. Yuh see, they stole my pardner last night. God knows where he is now. Me and him have been together a long time — a long time. Now, they got him — so I got Reynolds. He's my trade goods, ma'am, I'll turn him over to them in the same shape they turn Swede over to me."

"But where and how did you get Reynolds?"

Sad smiled at her. "There's a lot of things you don't know, ma'am."

"Come in and sit down, Sontag. I do not say that I believe you, but I am convinced that that letter is a hoax; so I'm willing to listen."

Sad followed her in and sat down.

"I'm glad of that," he told her. "Yuh see, that's the first time anybody around here, except Johnny Caldwell, has believed anythin' in my favor."

"I don't believe Johnny believes you now."

"Thasso? Yuh see, ma'am, he still believes in me, but he didn't want to go away, leavin' you in danger; so he kinda backslid, as yuh might say, in order to git a job with Uncle Hewie."

"Was that it?"

"Yes'm, that freckled-faced waddie thinks a heap of you."

Jean colored quickly and tried to change the subject.

"What was it you said about somebody stealing Harrigan?"

The expression of Sad's face changed in a flash.

"Yeah, they got him," softly. "Salt of the earth, that feller. Me and him have went through a lot in the last few years. Right now, if he's alive, he's jist waitin' for me to find him."

"But who got him, Sontag? The cattlemen wouldn't —"

"Jean Proctor, I'm goin' to tell yuh a few things. You prob'ly won't believe 'em, 'cause you won't want to believe 'em, but I'll tell yuh things yuh can't ignore, and after that —"

A sound at the dining room door caused Sad to turn his head quickly. A masked man was hunched in the doorway, covering him with a big Colt gun, another masked man crowding in behind him. Sad had barely time to look them over, when the sound of a shot crashed out, apparently just outside the kitchen door. Came a clatter of wood, the sound of a falling body.

"Keep yore hands still," hissed the man, advancing slowly. There was no time for Sad to even think of drawing a gun. The man came forward and took the gun from Sad's holster. Jean was leaning back in her chair, her eyes wide with fear and amazement.

"Ropes," growled the man with Sad's gun. "Git some of them towels in the kitchen."

177

"Why, what are you going to do?" asked Jean, frightened.

"Set still, ma'am," he warned in a husky voice. "If yuh behave, you won't git hurt none."

The two men were experts with a rope. Sad knew there must be a third man, who had remained outside the kitchen door, evidently on guard. Their arms were roped tightly, and the man prodded them outside. Sprawled near the kitchen door, lying across an armful of wood, was old Lightning.

"Oh, they've killed old Lightning!" cried Jean.

"Never mind him," growled the man.

"Better blindfold 'em," said the other, producing some dirty towels.

It was only a minute's work to blindfold them completely. Finally they were boosted into saddles, and the horses moved away with them.

It seemed to Sad that they rode for hours, before they finally stopped. They were taken off their horses and seated on the ground. Sad tried to talk with Jean, but his voice was muffled behind the towel, and he had no idea where she was.

Sad could feel the chill of sundown, and he surmised that it was about dark, when they were put in the saddle again and the cavalcade went on for about thirty minutes, when they were again taken from the saddle and entered a house. Their captors apparently talked in signs, because Sad was unable to distinguish any words. After another wait, they were taken down a narrow stairway, where Sad bumped his head on the way down.

178

He could smell a candle burning, as they forced him to sit down against a post to which they roped him.

Then the blindfold was removed and Sad blinked his eyes in Stygian blackness. A door creaked, a flash of starlight showed Sad that his captors had left by a stairway opening outside. It was only a flash, but Sad knew instinctively that he was in a cellar beneath a house.

"If we git enough folks down here, mebbe we can start a poker game," said Swede Harrigan's voice in the darkness.

Sad could hardly believe his ears.

"Swede, is that you?" he asked hoarsely.

"Well, now don't that beat hell by a hundred yards?" asked Swede. "Is that you, Sad?"

"What's left of me, pardner. Where are yuh?"

"I'm right here, tied to a post."

"Oh, I'm so glad you have found your pardner, Sontag," said Jean.

"You here, ma'am?" snorted Sad.

"I wish you would call me Jean."

"That's right — Jean. Are yuh all right?"

"Except my arms — they're both asleep."

Sad knew what she meant. His own arms were paining him.

"Now that we're all together, who got you, Swede?"

"Search me. You went into the depot, if yuh remember. A man came hurryin' up there, actin' like he was on business, and he walloped me over the head, I reckon. I seen plenty fireworks, I know that. And then I was on a horse, ridin' on my belly. I woke up pretty clear in the head, and I shore heard things. They wanted you too, but Stormy spoiled it. Didja know that?"

"Guessed it."

"Uh-huh. I didn't know their voices very well, but I know they've got a new scheme to put sheep in here. Bob Scott, the feller you mistreated, was one of 'em. He's a professional gun-man, and how he hates you! Bladen is an expert forger. He — say, there was somethin' about a letter to you from Reynolds. Bladen faked the postmarks."

"We know all about that letter," said Sad.

"Was that telegram a fake?" asked Jean.

"Shore was," replied Sad. "Steen had Reynolds send it."

"Well, what are we up against now?" wondered Swede.

"*Quien sabe?*" replied Sad. "I stole Reynolds last night, and he's in a safe place right now. That is, I hope he's safe."

"You — uh — you ain't jokin', are yuh, Sad?"

"Not a bit of it. I went down to the Flyin' M., knocked Terrill out with a six-gun barrel, and kidnapped Dan Reynolds."

"Well, you old son of a gun, you!"

"Do you mean to say that Steen is — is working for Reynolds?" asked Jean.

"First lieutenant," grunted Sad. "Welty was a Reynolds' man."

"But Dell Rios —"

"Check him in with the rest," dryly.

"Sontag, you don't mean to say — why, Dell Rios has as much at stake —"

"He shore puzzles me," said Sad.

"You say you found Reynolds at the Flying M?" asked Jean.

"Shore, he owns the ranch. Has owned it for a long time. And I've got a hunch he owns the Box A A, and the Lazy N Half Circle R. Reynolds was all set to give the word to bring in the sheep. Every man on the rim, except Welty, had helpless guns. I'll betcha the wires are cut on that dynamite warnin' and I wouldn't laugh out loud if yore big can of kerosene was water.

"But Reynolds got shot — and his sheepmen don't move without his personal orders. Welty got shot, and the boys found out about their dummy cartridges. That ended Reynolds' chances. We found out too much about their outfit and the crooks who were supposed to be cattlemen; so they schemed to put us out of commission. If they could prove we were connected with Reynolds, the cattlemen would either kill us off or run us out. Either way would suit the sheep interests. Caldwell knew it."

"And I didn't have enough brains to understand," sighed Jean.

"You trusted yore own men," said Sad. "I don't blame yuh. Mrs. Hewie Moore shore tried hard to believe us, but Hewie wouldn't. He's shore set in his ideas, Jean."

"I'd tell a man," chuckled Swede. "Anyway, what's the use of post-mortems, we've got to find a way out of this hole. Where have yuh got Reynolds?"

"That would be tellin'," replied Sad. "And walls have ears."

CHAPTER
FIFTEEN

It was Uncle Hewie Moore, who discovered the body of old Lightning. The old man had been shot through the heart, dying instantly, and it was apparent that someone in or near the kitchen door had shot down the old cook as he was bringing in an armful of wood.

Uncle Hewie was unable to find anyone else around the ranch, so he went to town as fast as his horse could travel, and notified the sheriff. Jean Proctor had not been to town that day, and the sheriff led the way back to the ranch, a fear in his heart that something had happened to her. Old Lightning had no enemies. Why would anyone shoot the old man down, except to seal his lips?

Johnny Caldwell rode in shortly after the sheriff and coroner had arrived, and they questioned him. But Johnny knew nothing. He told them he had come to tell Jean that he had examined the wiring on their dynamite signal and had found the wires cut and cleverly spliced with short pieces of wood, half way from the battery box to the charge. The five gallons of kerosene had been poured out some distance from the huge pyre of wood, and there only remained the empty can.

182

But Stormy was not interested in things on the rim, he wanted to know where Jean Proctor was. After things had been explained to Johnny he wanted the same information.

"I'd like to find Sontag," said Stormy.

"What's he got to do with this?" asked Johnny.

"I dunno, but I've got a hunch he came out here to-day."

"Was Swede with him?"

"Swede," said Stormy, "is missin'. Somebody got away with him last night."

Stormy proceeded to tell Johnny what he knew about it, and Johnny's blue eyes grew hard during the telling.

"And you think Sontag had anythin' to do with this killin'?" asked Johnny.

"Wouldn't put it past him," said Uncle Hewie, who had been silent during the whole talk.

Johnny snorted his disgust.

"Yuh ort to be on the rim," said Uncle Hewie.

"I know it. Rios' man never did come up there. Slim's goin' around lookin' for spooks, and Tony ain't any better."

"It's all right," said Hewie. "Reynolds has given up the idea of puttin' sheep across the rim. You bring Tony and Slim in with yuh, we'll need all of yuh for the round-up."

"What round-up, Uncle Hewie?"

"A buyer is takin' most everythin' off this range, and we've got to pull a big round-up of Bar 44, Two Bar J P, and the Circle R. We're awful short of men, but we'll git along."

"To hell with the cattle!" snorted Stormy. "We've got a murder and a missin' girl."

"She may show up," said the coroner. "Give her time."

"I'll go back and get the boys," said Johnny.

Time meant nothing to the three captives. They dozed fitfully, in spite of their benumbed condition, aching from the tight ropes, hungry and thirsty. They had no idea whether it was night or day. Their backs tied tightly to the posts, no chance to loosen the bonds.

For the first time in his life Sad was worried badly. Perhaps he realized their condition better than the rest. The men who had put them there would never dare to turn them loose.

There was no question in his mind that Reynolds' men were behind this scheme, although he felt sure Reynolds did not order it. He smiled grimly as he wondered what Dave Fowler would do. Would he get frightened and turn Reynolds loose? Sad would not blame him, if he did, when he found that Sad was missing.

Jean Proctor was game. No word of complaint passed her lips, but Sad knew how she was suffering.

To the three of them it seemed weeks before anyone came. It was two men, masked, heavily armed. They lighted a lantern and examined their captives. One of them chuckled at sight of Sad's bruised and swollen wrists.

"How about a little food and water?" asked Sad.

"Pretty soon." The man squatted on his heels and drew a square of paper from inside his shirt. Slowly he

184

unfolded it and held it where Sad could read it by the light of the lantern.

It was a reward notice, freshly printed, offering five thousand dollars reward for Sad Sontag, dead or alive. He was accused of murdering old Lightning and kidnapping Jean Proctor. The reward was offered by the county, and signed by the sheriff.

Sad laughed at the man, who folded the notice and replaced it inside his shirt.

"Fine chance of a conviction," said Sad.

"Ain't nothin' said about conviction, feller. It says 'dead or alive,' and yuh don't reckon we'll take yuh alive, do yuh?"

"What about the girl?"

"Now yo're talkin', Sontag. We'll trade yuh the girl for Reynolds."

"Trade *me* the girl?"

"You tell us where Reynolds is and we'll take the girl home."

Sad thought it over for a full minute.

"I'll tell yuh what I'll do. You take the girl to the Bar 44 and turn her over to Hewie Moore. Bring me a note from Hewie, saying that she is safe and well — and I'll tell yuh where to find Reynolds."

The man laughed mockingly. "And run all our necks into a noose, eh?"

"That's my trade — and I know Hewie's writin'."

"You poor fool! Don't yuh know that every man in this end of the valley is huntin' for that girl? And they're huntin' for you, Sontag. All we've got to do is

185

sock a bullet through you, pack yuh to town and collect the money. Don't worry — we'll collect."

"Will yuh? But not until yuh get Reynolds. And here's my ace-in-the-hole," lied Sad. "Reynolds is sufferin' as much as we are. I'm the only man who knows where he is — and a sheepman starves to death as quick as a cowpuncher. Roll that in a paper and smoke on it, you coyote."

"That's what I told yuh," growled the other masked man. "He couldn't git anybody to take care of Reynolds. I tell yuh, he had to rope Reynolds out in the brush."

"At least there's one man with brains in yore gang," said Sad.

"Didn't take much brains to figure that out," said Swede.

"And if Reynolds dies, you jiggers are out of luck," added Sad.

"I told yuh how we'd trade," reminded the man.

"And my proposition still stands," retorted Sad.

"We'll give yuh an answer later."

"How about a little food and water?"

"When Reynolds eats — you eat."

"Suits me. But this girl and my pardner never had any hand in it. Yuh don't need to starve them for what I done alone."

"That's right — but you won't git any, Sontag."

"I'm not askin' for any."

Since the day Sad Sontag had saved little Buddy's life, Dave Fowler had tried hard to keep the little fellow away from the main street. His usual playground was at the rear of the blacksmith shop, where his father could keep an eye on him. But to-day he worked his way around to the sidewalk near the Singing River Saloon.

Bill Steen came along and stopped to grin at the little fellow.

"How'r yuh comin', Buddy?" he asked.

"Pretty dood," said Buddy, smiling widely.

"Ain't tried to stop no more wild steers, have yuh?"

Buddy shook his head. "No more."

"That's fine. How's yore dad?"

"Awri'," twisting at a button on his overalls. Suddenly he looked up, his blue eyes wide, as he said:

"We dot cwazy man in our house."

"Yea-a-ah?" said Bill softly. "Crazy, eh? What made him crazy?"

"Me dunno."

"How do yuh know he's crazy?"

"My daddy tell me. He keep cwazy man locked up."

"Well, well!" A suspicion began to dawn upon Bill Steen. "How long has the crazy man been at yore house, Buddy?"

"Two nights."

"That's fine. Here," Bill gave Buddy a shiny quarter. "You go buy yourself some candy."

Bill walked past the blacksmith shop and saw that Fowler was busy nailing shoes on a horse. He went back to the hitch-rack and started to mount, as a horseman rode in from the south. Bill swore under his breath. The rider was Gale Reynolds drawn and pale, but determined of eye, as he drew up near Steen.

187

It was then that Bill noticed that Gale had a drawn revolver in his right hand, the muzzle projecting just beyond the swell-fork of his saddle. Steen knew that Gale had no speed on the draw, but he also knew that the kid could shoot straight.

"What in hell are you doin' up here?" asked Bill coldly.

Gale laughed shortly. "They are probably wondering the same thing at the Flying M. I'm not supposed to be able to get around, but this is once I fooled them. There will probably be consternation, when they find me gone, because I swore I'd come back here and finish telling what I started. Well, I'm here, Steen, and I'm going out to the Two Bar J P to tell what I know to Jean Proctor.

"You know what that means, don't you? I know a lot more to tell than I did before. I know you'll try to stop me. I picked this mare for her speed, and I rode slowly from the ranch, in case I needed speed. If you follow me, I'll shoot you, Steen; so your best bet is to get out of this country."

"I reckon I understand yuh," growled Steen. "Go ahead."

"Give me your gun — butt first."

The muzzle of that big Colt, braced against the saddle, covered Bill Steen's waist-line; so Bill Steen handed over his gun. Gale quickly drew out the cartridges, flung them into the street, threw the revolver far over against an old shed, and reined his horse back into the street.

188

"You poor fool!" gritted Bill, and went after his gun, which he cleaned and reloaded. Then he mounted his horse, rode a short way out of town, cut back and went straight to Fowler's home.

The front door was locked with a flimsy lock, which snapped off from Steen's weight. Another locked door resisted his efforts for a few moments, but a handy piece of drill steel solved that problem.

Dan Reynolds was lying on a bunk, tied hand and foot. His face was drawn, gray, but his eyes lighted up at sight of Steen, who quickly cut the ropes and helped Reynolds to his feet. Reynolds had not been tied tight enough to stop circulation.

"We've got to go easy," warned Steen. "Fowler's little kid gave it away. This is the last place we'd ever think of lookin'."

They went to a front window and peered out.

"What's new?" asked Reynolds in a tired voice.

"Hell's poppin', Dan. We've got Sontag and Harrigan, all tied up."

"Good work!"

"And we've got Jean Proctor."

"You've got Jean Proctor? What do you mean, Bill?"

"We've got the three of 'em — together. And hell's turned loose for noon. They think Sontag kidnapped her and killed the old cook at the Two Bar J P. There's a five thousand dollar reward for Sontag — dead or alive."

"You mean — that girl was kidnapped?"

"Yeah."

"By whose orders?"

Bill shrugged his shoulders. "It jist happened, I suppose."

"I'll *get* somebody for that mistake."

"Wait a minute. Sontag convinced her of everythin' he knew. We had to shut her mouth. He proved that the letter from you was faked. Here's the latest — Gale got away, came through here a while ago, got the drop on me, and told me he was goin' out to tell Jean Proctor the truth. The poor fool won't find anybody there."

"Won't he? Suppose he finds someone there from the Bar 44. They'll believe him. And if he don't find anybody there, he'll come back here to Singing River, and find plenty to believe him."

"I'll see that he don't."

"All right, Bill; but if you hurt him — you answer to me. He's my son, even if he don't act like it — and I want him."

"All right. You go out the back way, head straight west and hide in that big mesquite clump at the head of that crooked arroya. I'll see that yuh have a horse before dark."

Steen thought he had been unobserved, but he reckoned without little Buddy Fowler, who had reached the rear gate as Reynolds left the kitchen door and hurried away from town. Little Buddy saw Steen mount his horse and ride the opposite direction. His childish mind did not entirely grasp the situation, but he knew it was wrong for those men to be in his home when no one else was there.

So he wandered back to the blacksmith shop and watched the sparks fly from the anvil. Finally his father tossed the hot iron into the water of the slack-tub, wiped his grimy hands on his leather apron and smiled fondly at the golden haired youngster.

"Man go to our house," said Buddy seriously. "One, two man."

Fowler's smile faded. "What men, Buddy?"

"Big man give me money."

"Big man?" Dave Fowler scowled thoughtfully. He had seen Steen in town. "You mean Mr. Steen?"

Buddy nodded quickly. "He have horse. One man walk."

Fowler yanked off his apron and flung it aside.

"Are yuh sure yuh saw two men, Buddy?" he asked.

"See two man."

"You stay right here in the shop," ordered his father. "I'll be back in a minute."

Fowler's fears were realized, when he found the broken locks, the cut ropes. Bill Steen had released Reynolds — why? He hurried back to the shop and questioned the youngster. Did Steen take Reynolds away with him? Buddy was rather vague, except that Steen went away on his horse, and the other man walked away. Apparently they went different directions.

It made rather a tough situation for Fowler. Here was everybody in the country trying to capture or kill Sontag, who had captured Reynolds, who had been released by Steen. Fowler couldn't understand it. If Sontag was working for Reynolds, why would he capture his boss? If Steen was a cattleman, why would he release Reynolds and let him go? Everyone was saying that Sontag had killed Lightning and kidnapped

Jean Proctor. Dave Fowler leaned against his forge and tried to reason all this out.

Finally he made his decision, and walked straight across the street to the sheriff's office, where he found Tiny Parker, trying to fit a new firing-pin in his rifle.

"Whatcha got on yore mind, Dave?" he asked.

Fowler was no story teller, and in a few words he told Tiny what had happened. Tiny forgot his firing-pin. He rolled a cigarette, put it in his pocket, threw the sack of tobacco in a cuspidor and put the match in his mouth.

"That's shore as hell remarkable," he told Fowler. "Are yuh shore it was Dan Reynolds?"

"Sontag said it was. The man offered me a thousand dollars to turn him loose."

"Grades himself pretty high," said Tiny.

Tiny didn't know just what to do about it, so he went hunting for Stormy. He found the sheriff with Farraday, and blurted out what Fowler had told him. The two men were interested, and Stormy was puzzled.

"This here thing is gittin' to be more of a Chinese puzzle every day," complained Stormy. "Damn Sontag! He shore raised hell and put a chunk under it when he came to this country. I can't git m' mind set about him, Jim. If he kidnapped Reynolds — why would he murder old Lightnin' and steal Jean Proctor? If he ain't Reynolds' man — well, I'm a liar if I know what to think."

"Why would Bill Steen turn Reynolds loose?" asked Tiny.

"My Gawd, you don't make it any easier for me, do yuh!" snorted the exasperated sheriff. "I reckon I'll go

192

and ask Bill Steen. Tiny, you stay around the office and keep Sontag from stealin' that, will yuh?"

Tiny promised to save at least the foundation. Farraday watched the sheriff ride out of Singing River. His eyes were gloomy, as he muttered to himself:

"I suppose I should have cut in ahead of the sheriff and warned Bill Steen, but I'm gettin' so damn leary of the whole thing that I'll jist set still and let Steen do his own lyin'."

CHAPTER
SIXTEEN

Johnny Caldwell was thoroughly and miserably down-hearted. He had ridden with the sheriff's posse, ridden with Slim and Tony as a three-man searching party, and now he was sitting on the steps of the Two Bar J P ranch-house, chin in his hands, wondering what to do next. There was no one else at the ranch. As a matter of fact, Johnny had come over there to — well, a sort of vague idea of forcing Bill Steen to tell what he knew. No definite plan, of course. But Bill was not at the ranch.

Johnny wasn't interested in the round-up of Bar 44 cattle. In fact, no one seemed interested in gathering cattle for Clinton. The shooting of old Lightning and the disappearance of Jean Proctor had halted the plans of Clinton to clean out the range — much to his disgust. He pleaded with Uncle Hewie, but the old man told him he'd bunch cows when Jean Proctor was found. Apparently the Circle R outfit felt the same about it, and the Two Bar J P had not gathered a single head.

Johnny lifted his head and squinted his blue eyes against the sun. A rider was coming in from toward town. Johnny shifted the position of his gun. If this was Bill Steen, Bill was in a fair way to explain a few things.

But it was not Bill Steen. Johnny did not recognize the horse, and he did not recognize the rider, until the man was only a few yards away.

It was Gale Reynolds. Johnny's right hand sagged down to the top of his holster, and his eyes hardened.

"Hello, Caldwell," said Gale in a weary voice.

"Howdy, feller," coldly. "What are you doin' here?"

Gale slowly dismounted and came over to the steps. His skin was sallow, his eyes dark-rimmed. He leaned against the railing for a few moments and sat down.

"Is Miss Proctor home?" he asked.

Johnny looked him over queerly. "You know damn well she ain't."

"No, I didn't know it, Caldwell. Where is she?"

Johnny's lips tightened for a moment. Then:

"Are you lyin' or are yuh jis downright damn ignorant?"

"Probably ignorant," said Gale slowly. "You see, I've been down and out quite a while. To-day I sneaked away and came here."

There might be truth in that, decided Johnny; so he told Gale what had happened; the disappearance of Swede Harrigan, the murder of old Lightning, disappearance of Jean and Sontag. Gale listened blankly.

"I don't blame you for thinking I was lying," said Gale. "I met Bill Steen in Singing River, and told him I was coming out here to see Miss Proctor. But he didn't say a word about her being missing — just let me come ahead."

"He probably would," nodded Johnny. "Funny feller, Bill is."

"And rather dangerous," smiled Gale. "You see, I have a strong idea that our friend Bill Steen shot me that night. They told me Sontag did it."

"Yea-a-a-ah?" Johnny played ignorant. "Why would Bill shoot you?"

Gale laughed shortly. "There's a lot of things you don't know, Caldwell. However, that is past. Right now, I'd like to know where Miss Proctor is."

"They're offerin' five thousand dollars for Sad Sontag, dead or alive."

Gale laughed wearily. "I'd like to meet him. It seems to me he'd be worth knowing."

"Y'betcha."

"They were in our home in San Francisco the night my father got shot," said Gale. "There was a wreck of two taxi-cabs, and they brought Dad home. I never did get the straight of it. Anyway, I arrived home from here that night. Dad left them in the library and came in to see me.

"Well, we had it hot and heavy. He told me I ought to be shot, and I asked him to try and do it. Oh, I guess we were both hot. Our butler has always hated me — he's one of Dad's gang — and I knew he was listening. There came a shot through the doorway, and Dad went down. He had his hand in his coat pocket, and as he went down he drew his gun.

"I drew my gun and ran outside to see if I could find the man who shot him, and while I was out there in the rain, falling over shubbery, Sontag and Harrigan left

196

the place. The butler swore they shot him, but Dad said they didn't. Later the butler told me he tried to incriminate the two cowboys to save me, because he was sure I shot Dad. I guess he still believes it — but I don't care."

Johnny sighed deeply. "If I was you, I'd pull out, before somebody crowned yuh Queen of May."

"No, I don't believe I shall."

"Write yore own ticket," said Johnny wearily, as he got to his feet.

Gale walked over to his horse.

"I'm going to stop and have a talk with Dell Rios," he said.

"You've got my permission, Reynolds."

"I wasn't asking for your permission."

"Take it along, anyway," said Johnny dryly.

The sun was nearly down over the western range, when Bill Steen, leading an extra saddle horse, found Dan Reynolds in the mesquite.

"It took you a long time to bring me a horse," complained Reynolds.

"Yo're damn lucky to git one any time," growled Steen, handing the reins to Reynolds. "Let's get to hell out of here — fast."

Reynolds was willing, and they galloped several miles toward the Flying M., before Steen offered any information.

"Fowler's kid saw me and you leave their house," said Bill. "He told his father, and the sheriff got the information."

"Well?" queried Reynolds.

"Not so damn well — not the way things are. I went out to the Circle R to git you this horse, and that fool son of yours came along. I got the drop on him, and I was goin' to bring him along, when the sheriff showed up. The kid took advantage of it, backed into the house, where Scott bounced a gun off his head. He's plenty safe now.

"But I shore had a sweet time, tryin' to prove to the sheriff that I never turned you loose. I said I thought Sontag was in Fowler's house, but somebody broke in and took him away before I got there. It was a slick lie, but I don't believe Stormy believed me. Clinton ain't havin' any luck with the round-up, 'cause everybody is lookin' for Jean Proctor. And do you realize that the sheep are due to come in over the rim, day after tomorrow?"

"I know they are. Never mind Clinton. If they're all searchin' for that girl, we're sitting pretty. But what about Gale? You say he —"

"Jist a tap on the head; he's all right."

"That's a hell of a way for a man to treat his own son," bitterly. "I wish I had never seen a damn sheep! Steen, have you brains enough to realize what we're up against? Every one of us has our heads in a loop right now."

"That girl — yuh mean?"

"Nothing less. She knows everything that Sontag knows, and he knows about everything. We can't let her loose — we can't let Sontag and Harrigan loose. Don't you see what we're up against?"

"Leave that to us, Dan. I've got a scheme."

198

"You've had a lot of 'em — you and Bladen."

"Bladen is no fool, Dan."

"No, and he's the crookest crook on earth — a dope-crook. Had a wonderful training in surgery, but his brain is crooked."

"Why do yuh keep him around?"

"Because I need him. Cleverest forger in the country. I had to ship him out of Frisco. What do you figure on doing with Sontag?"

"Why?"

"Curiosity. You see, he saved my life — and I owe him something."

"After the things he's done against yuh — yo're even."

"Maybe. It's all in the point of view, Bill. I'd like to give him a break."

"And get all of us hung."

"Yes, that's true."

After a meal at the ranch, Reynolds was so worn out that he went to bed. Steen, Terrill and Bladen got together in the main room and had a few drinks. Everything had been explained, and the seriousness of the situation talked over.

"For a thin dime, Dan would pull out on us," said Steen. "He's scared over that girl, and he's gettin' chicken-hearted over Sontag. This is no time to git yeller, boys. Day after tomorrow the sheep come in over the rim, and we'll hold Dan to the bonus he promised."

Bladen smiled thoughtfully. "Getting yellow, eh? Yes, I think he might. Well, suppose he does?"

Bladen's eyes were unnaturally bright, as he drew a legal-looking document from his pocket and spread it under the light of the lamp.

It was a bill-of-sale for the Flying M and everything thereon, made out in favor of Charles H. Bladen, and signed with the flowing hand of Reynolds, whose signature was very distinctive. It had been witnessed by Terrill and Lentz.

"Well, I'll be damned!" snorted Steen. "Where did you git enough money to buy this outfit, Doc?"

Bladen smiled and drew out another bill of sale, witnessed by the same men, in which he was the purchaser of every head of sheep bearing the mark of Dan Reynolds. Steen looked at him in amazement.

"And that signature will even fool Dan Reynolds," said Bladen.

"You mean, you —" Steen blinked at Bladen.

"Do you think I'm a millionaire?" sneered Bladen.

"That's my signature," said Terrill. "But I never —"

"Stop yellin'," warned Steen. He turned to Bladen. "Now, where do we come in on this deal, Doc?"

"I get a half," coldly. "You and Terrill split the other half."

"But — but what about Dan?" asked Steen in a whisper.

"Use your imagination."

Steen's hand was shaking as he reached for the bottle.

"Doc., yo're a wonder."

"But who — how do we —" Terrill jerked his thumb toward the closed door of Reynolds' room.

200

"Fits perfectly with Steen's scheme for the rest of the bunch," smiled Bladen.

"What is that?" asked Terrill.

Bladen leaned across the table and whispered softly into Terrill's ear. Terrill's ferret-like face turned a pasty gray, as he leaned back, staring at Bladen. His little brown eyes shifted to Steen's big face and back to the bright eyes of Doc. Bladen.

"Christ!" he snorted softly. "Give me that bottle."

"That'll give us a clean slate," said Steen.

"What about the rest of the boys?" queried Terrill nervously.

"We'll take care of those we pick out," said Bladen. "It's thumbs-down for some of 'em."

Terrill downed another big glass of raw liquor, and it brought the colour back to his face.

"We'll all be rich," he said huskily. "I'll take mine and go to Mexico City. Lotta senoritas down there. Better come along with me, Bill?"

Bill Steen laughed hoarsely. "I've allus wanted to see Paris."

"You're both drunk," said Bladen. "Go to bed, Terrill."

"Ain't you goin' to stay here all night, Bill," asked Terrill.

"Bill is going back, to see that everything goes right." said Bladen. "We can't overlook a single bet now."

"Tha's ri'," mumbled Terrill. "Lo's senoritas down there, Bill. You better go with me."

CHAPTER
SEVENTEEN

It was a haggard bunch of prisoners in that old cellar, dimly illuminated by a smoky lantern, which hung from a dirty beam. Their faces were white, where they were not streaked from dirt and perspiration. They had long since ceased to try and loosen their bonds.

Jean and Swede had received food and water, but none had been given to Sad. They had barely touched it, although Sad had begged them to go ahead and eat.

"Somethin' will break for us, and yuh need strength," he said.

"I can't eat it," protested Jean.

Two masked men had attended the feeding. One would release their hands, while the other sat against the door, guarding them with a shot-gun. Neither of the men could be drawn into conversation. Sad wanted to know what time it was and what day, but they refused to tell him.

There was a break in the monotony, when the limp form of Gale Reynolds was brought in and roped to an upright. One of the men threw a cup of cold water in his face, before they went away. For quite a while Gale was dazed, but he gradually recovered enough to talk with them.

His stock of information was of little value to them, except that he was able to tell them the day of the week, and the approximate time when he was knocked out. He told them of his conversation with Johnny Caldwell and Bill Steen.

"Well, the sheep are not in yet," said Sad.

"No, they're not," agreed Gale.

"Are yuh sure we're at the Circle R?" asked Swede.

"That's where I was, the last thing I knew."

"Dell Rios must be in with the gang," said Swede.

"I don't want to believe that," said Jean. "I can't see why Dell would do a thing like that."

"You had plenty faith in Bill Steen," reminded Swede.

"She had a perfect right to have faith in him," said Sad.

"Thank you, Sad," said Jean weakly. "You have a forgiving disposition."

"I've made a lot of fool mistakes in my life, Jean."

"Yeah, and this one looks like the last," grunted Swede.

"Does look a little cloudy, pardner; but every cloud has a silver linin'. Dyin' ain't so bad, but I do hate to die on an empty stummick."

"Oh, you must be simply starving!" said Jean pityingly.

"No, ma'am — jist cured of eatin'."

"What are they going to do with all of us?" wondered Gale.

"One guess is as good as another," replied Sad.

It was an hour or so later, when the men came with food, and it was rather a surprise, when they released Sad's hands and let him eat.

"Reynolds is loose," said one of the masked men huskily. "He was found in Fowler's house in Singin' River."

"All right," replied Sad, as he ate ravenously. "That don't worry me."

"No, you ain't got nothin' to worry about," said the man meaningly.

They waited until everyone had finished their meal, tied their wrists again and went away.

"What did he mean by that last remark, Sad?" asked Swede.

"Oh, I reckon he meant that they'd take good care of me. Gosh, that stuff tasted good! Now, I'm all set to do a little thinkin' again."

"I'd like to be loose and have five minutes with my father," said Gale bitterly.

"So would I," chuckled Sad. "But yo're safe, young feller. He won't hurt you none."

"Why would he hurt any of you? I feel sure he is merely keeping you here until he gets the sheep over the rim."

"Thank yuh," dryly. "I hope yo're right, Reynolds."

Johnny Caldwell started back to the Bar 44, after Gale Reynolds had ridden away from the Two Bar J P, but after going a ways Johnny turned and rode back toward town. At the forks of the road he met Stormy See, who had been to the Circle R.

"Whatcha know, Stormy?" asked Johnny.

"Not very much, Caldwell."

"Didja see Gale Reynolds over at the Circle R?"

"No, was he supposed to be there?"

Johnny told about meeting him at the Two Bar J P.

"I saw Bill Steen," admitted the sheriff, after Johnny told him what Gale had said. And then Stormy told Johnny about the escape of Dan Reynolds. Johnny was rather amazed.

"I'll betcha forty dollars Bill Steen lies," said Johnny. "He knows he lies, the damned coyote. Thought the little kid meant Sontag! Stormy, I hope to notch a sight on Bill Steen before this is over. Didja see Dell Rios?"

"Yeah, I saw Dell. He ain't so awful well, I don't reckon. Looks like he's been sick."

They rode on to town, where Johnny questioned Fowler. There was no question in Fowler's mind that Steen had turned Reynolds loose. The town was rather quiet that night. Johnny Caldwell, with a few dollars in his pocket, got into a poker game and stayed there until three o'clock in the morning.

As he was riding back toward the Bar 44 in the moonlight, he saw the silhouette of a rider against the sky, crossing over a tall ridge, traveling north. Johnny drew up his horse, wondering who would be cutting across the hills at that time of the morning, and he saw eleven more riders top the same ridge, all travelling the same direction.

"And that," said Johnny out loud, "beats hell — easy. A dozen men, ridin' this early!"

But they were gone now, and there was only the tall ridge, silvered with moonlight. Johnny shook his head and went on to the Bar 44, where he climbed into bed, determined to try and trail those riders after daylight.

But Johnny overslept and only arose in time for breakfast. Slim Reed and Tony Rush were there. Slim hadn't gone back to the Two Bar J P after old Lightning had been murdered. He would have quit his job, except that there was no one to pay him what money he had coming. He and Tony were tired of riding all over the country, searching for Jean Proctor.

Uncle Hewie was becoming crabbed over things. He wanted to sell those cattle to Clinton, but he was willing to sacrifice the chance in order to spend the time in searching.

"If you'd only believed in Sontag," complained Johnny at the breakfast table.

Uncle Hewie snorted disgustedly. "Yea-a-ah! And them offerin' five thousand dollars for him, dead or alive."

"It's a big mistake," stubbornly. "Sontag never stole Jean. I'm scared he's been killed — him and Harrigan."

"What about Jean Proctor?" asked Slim.

Johnny shut his eyes tightly for several moments, got up from the table and went down to the corral.

"You've got a lot of sense," said Uncle Hewie.

"I never thought," replied Slim. "But, hell, we're as anxious as he is, the danged fire-eater. I tell yuh, Hewie, I ain't believed things, but right now I'm willin' to force a showdown. If Bill Steen is what Johnny says he is, I'm for picklin' Bill in a barrel of brine."

206

"More Sontag!" snorted Hewie, but he followed Johnny down to the corral, where Johnny was saddling his horse.

"Where yuh goin'?" asked Hewie.

"I seen twelve men ridin' over the ridge in the moonlight this mornin'," said Johnny, yanking savagely on his latigo. "And I'm goin' to see where they went. Lend me a rifle, will yuh?"

Hewie scratched his head thoughtfully, eyes half-closed.

"No-o-o-o, I don't mind lendin' yuh a rifle, Johnny. How'd it be if I loaned a rifle to Slim and Tony and me — and we went along?"

Johnny looked keenly at the old cattleman.

"You ain't backslidin' on yore inner fellin's, are yuh, Hewie?"

"No-o-o-o," drawled the old man dryly, "but I'd like a good scrap. Idy's been a-ridin' me quite a lot."

"She believes in Sontag, Hewie."

"Hell, kid, you ain't a-tryin' to tell me somethin', are yuh? No? I'll call Slim and Tony."

As he bow-legged his way back to the house, Johnny Caldwell grinned widely for the first time in several days.

There were three men in a small room, apparently a crudely furnished bedroom. Roped to a chair, his back to the wall, was Dan Reynolds, looking years older than he had even when Steen released him. Standing against the wall near the door was Dell Rios. Beside a little table in the center of the room, the top bare of everything, except a bottle and two glasses, was Doc. Bladen, his eyes glassy, a sneer on his lips.

"I still don't quite get your scheme," said Reynolds.

"No?" Bladen leered at him. "Ignorance won't get you anything, Dan. You've seen the two bills of sale, and I'm gambling that nobody will ever question those signatures. Tomorrow morning the sheep come in over the rim — my sheep, damn you. Oh, I've already sent wires and letters to your men. They *know* I've bought you out. Nobody around here will ever know where you went, nor will they care."

Reynolds sighed softly, gnawing at a corner of his lips. He realized that Bladen was perfectly capable of carrying out the scheme. His eyes shifted to Dell Rios' grim face. No help in that quarter, and he knew it.

"You will take the big split, I suppose, Doc.," he said.

"Why not? I'm shooting for a lifetime stake."

"You better quit using dope, if you want to live to enjoy it."

Bladen laughed harshly.

"What about Sontag — and that girl?" asked Reynolds.

"Never mind them. Why not ask about your son?"

The lines of Reynolds' face deepened. "You might give the kid an even break."

"You didn't."

"Guilty," Reynolds shook his head wearily. "I don't see why I ever befriended you, Doc. Unless I'm mistaken, you were going to put me out of the game a long time ago."

Bladen laughed. "Right. You should have been at the bottom of the Pacific — but Sontag —"

"I thought so. One of your men died, the other, a cripple for life."

"That doesn't matter. All that matters now is that I've won the game."

Bladen laughed and got to his feet. "I'm leavin' you here along with a particular friend of yours, Dan."

Bladen left the room, and Dell Rios took the chair, placing it near the door. Reynolds looked him over gloomily.

"Well, Rios, I suppose you're happy."

"I ought to be, Reynolds."

"I suppose you should. Too bad you didn't make a good job of it in Frisco."

Rios' eyes blinked quickly. "You knew it, eh?"

"Guessed it — after I knew you were there. Afraid I'd talk, eh?"

"No, damn yuh, I was tryin' to save this range."

"Yes? And just how would that save it?"

"Muddle things up long enough for me to come back and kill one more man."

Reynolds smiled wearily. "I see. Not a bad scheme."

"At least, when this is over, *you* won't hold any club over me."

"That's true. But, Rios, you know there is an old saying — murder will out."

"Not in this case."

"No? And just how are things to be disposed of?"

Rios reached in his pocket and drew out a match. Snapping it to a blaze on the edge of his thumbnail, he held it up, until it burned out. Reynolds knew what Rios meant. He thought it over carefully.

"Isn't there a five thousand dollar reward for Sontag?"

Rios nodded quickly. "Dead or alive. We collect on him."

"At least, that's a favour to him."

Rios nodded indifferently.

"You're a queer person, Rios," said Reynolds slowly. "Right now your insides are all upset over this thing. You are not a natural killer. You'll never be able to look another man in the face, and you'll always be looking behind you. Money won't help you any. It's true, I will be marked off the list, but — wasn't there a time when you thought a lot of that girl?"

Rios got to his feet and came closer to Reynolds, eyes blazing.

"Keep yore tongue off that," he warned. "Damn you, I've heard that from you before — when you held the whip."

"Keep your temper, Rios. I've no cause to be loyal to anybody now. Have you got a pencil and paper in your pocket?"

Rios produced an old note-book and a short piece of lead pencil.

"Move that table over closer," said Reynolds. "I believe I've got enough slack in this rope to write what I want to write."

It was a difficult position, but luckily the table was low enough for the purpose. With his bound hands on the tabletop, Reynolds wrote rapidly for a space of time, dropped the pencil back on the table and settled back in his chair. Dell Rios picked up the note-book and read what Reynolds had written. His eyes opened widely and his unshaven jaw sagged weakly for a moment.

"Reynolds, is this true?" he asked shakily.

"As true as I am alive, Rios."

"Good God! And you — you —"

"I had the whip hand, Rios."

Dell sat down in his chair, holding his head in his hands for a long time, and when he looked up his eyes were wet.

"Thank yuh, Reynolds," he said huskily. "Better late than never."

"That's all right. I wish I could square up some of my other deals as easy as that."

"I wish —" Rios hesitated, staring at the floor. A man wearing a mask, came to the door.

"I'll stay here," he said. "They want yuh downstairs."

"What time is it, Rios?" asked Reynolds. Rios looked at his watch.

"A little after four," he replied, as the door closed behind him.

He stopped outside the room and adjusted a black mask, before going down the stairs.

The four men from the Bar 44 had circled the entire rim, riding their weary way around, in hopes of cutting the trail of the twelve riders, and finally stopped at the Two Bar J P. There was no one at home; so they proceeded to enter the kitchen and cook a meal of ham and eggs, with plenty of strong coffee.

"I think you was dreamin' about them riders," said Slim; as they drifted away from the ranch.

"I seen 'em," declared Johnny. "I wasn't drunk either. Let's work down across the hills to the Circle R."

So they spread out again and began working the hills, always looking for the sign left by twelve horses. If they rode in single file or bunched, it might be possible to trail them.

Just north of the Circle R ranch buildings was a deep washout, where, at some remote time a cloudburst had riven a great hole in the earth. This had grown up with willows and a few stunted cottonwoods. And it was in this washout that Johnny made a discovery. There were twelve saddled horses, all tied to one long, heavy rope, which had been strung between three cottonwoods.

He caught the rest of the boys and took them down there. The animals bore the brands of the Flying M, Lazy N Half Circle R, and the Box A A.

"But what does it mean?" wondered Uncle Hewie.

"The sheepmen, I'll betcha," said Slim. "Hewie, them sheep are due to hit the rim danged soon, I tell yuh. This here bunch is in here to do battle with us, if we try to stop the sheep."

"Mebbe you'll believe now," said Johnny. "Sontag swore to me that Dan Reynolds owns the Flyin' M, and he said he'd bet he owns the Lazy N Half Circle R, and the Box A A. He's got his whole gang here."

Hewie's jaw jutted belligerently and he fingered his rifle.

"And," warned the cautious Tony, "I'd hate like hell to have 'em find me down here in this hole."

They went back to their horses and sat down in the brush away from the edge of the washout.

"We can't stay here," decided Uncle Hewie. "If there's any truth in what Sontag told you, Johnny; and if them twelve riders are in here to keep us from blockin' the sheep — we've got to git busy."

"Let's go to town and scrape up every man we can find," suggested Slim.

"Right now," said Johnny. "And let's move fast. We'll swing wide, so none of 'em will see us."

There were at least a dozen men in that big room, when Sad Sontag was led up from the cellar blindfolded. The curtains were drawn and the light was dim, as the cloth was removed from his eyes. The men were all masked, all looked alike.

No one spoke, as Sad blinked around at them. Near him, on the table was his own cartridge belt and holstered gun. He rubbed his wrists, after the ropes were taken away, paying no attention to the men, who had left him standing near the table. Finally one of them arose and came over near him. Before the man opened his mouth Sad knew it was Doc. Bladen.

"Sontag, your case has been passed upon," said Bladen, making no effort to disguise his voice. "For a certain service rendered some time ago, you are to go free."

213

"That's nice of yuh," said Sad slowly.

"No thanks to me," said Bladen evenly. "You will be given a horse and your own gun. It will require about ten or twelve hours for you to reach a town north of here — and that is the direction you will take."

Sad nodded, his eyes shifting to his gun.

"Sit down," ordered Bladen indicating a chair. Sad sat down. From the light through the windows he could see that it was almost sundown.

The council had apparently broken up, as several of the men had left the room. Sad's jaw tightened. He knew what was going to happen. They were going to give him a horse and a gun — a gun loaded with dummy shells — and they were going to shoot him down to collect the reward. Never for a moment had he been fooled. They would never dare let him go, not with what he knew about them.

His mind was working fast. Go to the north. That meant to go away from Singing River. He knew this was the Circle R ranch-house, and he searched his memory for the layout of buildings. To the south, and a little to the left was the big stable. North — what was to the north? An old log building on one side, sheds on the other. He would pass between them.

His mind was never more keen. He knew what he was going to do. It was a long shot chance — a chance that might work, if those men thought for a moment that he was fooled by their offer. If not, it would not matter. His eyes shifted to that good old Colt on the table. It was worthless as a weapon, loaded as it was. But Sad knew something that no one else knew, except

Swede, and Swede had often laughed at Sad over it. The last thing Sad had heard as they led him from the cellar was Swede's low-voiced, "Keep grinnin', pardner."

It was Swede's way of saying good-bye. He had heard a sob from Jean Proctor. He felt the surge of returning strength in his sore arms and wrists, and his lips drew back in a wolfish grin. The gods of chance were giving him a break again; a chance to win or lose in action. His plan was clear. Bladen came back.

"All ready, Sontag?" he asked.

"All set," said Sad, as he got to his feet. "Much obliged."

"There's your gun, Sontag — your horse is ready."

Slowly he buckled the old belt around him. He held out his hand to Bladen, but it was ignored.

"Keep going north," said Bladen, "and never come back, Sontag."

"I'm no fool," replied Sad.

"Try and live up to it."

CHAPTER
EIGHTEEN

Sad walked slowly outside through the kitchen door. There was no one in sight. A mocking-bird called from the ridge of the house, and a few chickens scratched around the yard. The horse was tied at the kitchen door — the blood-bay, branded with the Box A A; the horse Bob Scott had ridden to Singing River. It was the same saddle, too. Sad saw it all at a glance.

This rather added to their scheme. They would probably kill the blood-bay, too, making out that Sad had stolen the animal. It snorted, as Sad came up to it and untied the reins. The road to Singing River led slightly to the right from in front of the house. To the left, a hundred yards away and down a slight slope was the big stable.

Sad's jaw shut tightly, as he turned the horse around, heading north. He drew a rein tight, as he made a weak effort to put his foot in the saddle, and the horse began turning. This movement put him on the opposite side of the horse from Bladen, and as the animal made the half turn, Sad jabbed him in the flank with his clenched hand.

The half-wild animal snorted with fright, lunged ahead, broke into a wild gallop, with Sad grasping the

216

stirrup and heading the horse straight toward the stable. The movement was so unlooked for that there was not a sound from anyone, until the horse and running man were almost at the stable.

Somewhere a man yelled a warning, a bullet tore up the dirt just past Sad's running feet, and almost at the same moment Sad let loose. He fell, turned over twice, got to his feet and stumbled into the stable, as another bullet splintered through the wall over his head. He raced down the stable, darted in behind a stall and jerked out his gun. Quickly he removed the cartridges, and then he did a curious thing. Taking hold of the bottom of his old vest, he forcibly tore away the lining on one side, disclosing six discoloured .45 calibre cartridges.

It was his private *cache*. Six on each side. He told Swede he wore them there to keep his vest from getting out of shape.

Swiftly he loaded the gun. A man had appeared at the doorway of the stable. Peering through the cracks of the stall, Sad could see him, coming boldly along. It was a tall man, masked in black. There were no preliminaries.

Sad stepped out and fired from his hip. They were not over ten feet apart. The man went down in a sprawling heap, falling half way into a stall. Sad jerked off his mask, but the man was a stranger. He wore a black shirt, worn overalls, a black sombrero. Sad's shirt was dark.

Swiftly he adjusted the mask, put on the black hat. The man's gun and belt went around Sad's waist, Sad's gun went inside his own shirt, and Sad's belt and holster went into the manger. Stooping quickly, he picked up the man and dumped him into a deep manger, where no one could see him from the runway.

It was all done swiftly, and only a short time had elapsed from the shot, until Sad ran outside, around the corner, where he leaned against the wall, gun in hand.

There were men all around the stable.

"Didja git him, Renn?" asked one of them.

Renn! In a flash Sad remembered that Renn was supposed to be the owner of the Box A A. Sad's voice was muffled behind his mask.

"Git, hell! He's got a loaded gun."

Bladen laughed harshly. "Loaded gun! Go in and get him. He hasn't any loaded cartridges."

"He shot splinters in my face," mumbled Sad. "He's got a loaded gun."

"Go back to the house, you yaller pup!" snarled Bladen. "A couple of you fellows go in there and down him. He can't hurt you."

Sad accepted the rebuke and went slowly toward the house. Bladen laughed sneeringly, while two men went cautiously into the stable.

Bob Scott was standing in the kitchen doorway, as Sad came up. He had heard what Bladen said. He had removed his mask.

"Scared of a blank ca'tridge, eh?" he sneered.

"He's got loads," muttered Sad. "Can't fool me."

"Better git under cover," sneered Scott, and stepped aside, backing just inside the house.

That move was Scott's undoing. Before he had time to realize that anything was wrong, the supposed Renn had drawn a gun and slashed him over the head with it. For once in his life Sad Sontag did not, as they say in ring parlance, pull his punch. He slashed Scott with every ounce of strength, and the big Colt bit deeply.

He caught Scott in his arms and staggered over to the trap door of the kitchen. He flung back the door and dropped Scott. He heard a warning yell from the stable. They had found Renn. Swiftly he dropped into the cellar and let the trap door back into place.

The white faces of the prisoners were turned toward him, wondering what had happened, and Sad almost cried out at sight of Swede, who dug into Scott's pockets, where he found a pocket-knife. It was only a matter of a few moments to cut away the ropes. There was no explanations, no questions. Sad gave Swede Scott's gun and belt, and to Gale he gave his own (Sad's) gun.

"The silver lining," whispered Jean hoarsely.

"Painted by Sad Sontag," gritted Swede. "Are yuh all right, Sad?"

"As good as ever and gittin' better."

"Who was it yuh dumped in here?"

"Friend Scott, the tough *hombre* from the Panhandle."

They could hear the men tramping on the floor overhead. Sad stepped over on the ladder, trying to get an ear as close as possible to the edge of the trap door. Someone was calling Scott's name, others were cursing in no uncertain terms.

Doc. Bladen was acting like a madman. They had discovered the body of Renn in the manger, and now they realized that Sad Sontag was loose, with Renn's gun. Bladen wanted to know who was the traitor who gave Sontag the loaded cartridges; but there was no reply, because Bladen had loaded the gun himself, not trusting anyone.

"Mebbe he bushed Renn and shot him with his own gun," suggested one of the men.

"Damn Scott!" roared Bladen. "Where is he? Can't I trust anybody around here? Sontag is loose and hell is to pay."

"He can't git away on foot," said one of the men.

"Can't he? He'd go north — on foot. Better cover. A couple of you get out to the horses! If he ever finds that remuda —"

Two of the men went racing from the house, while Bladen paced the floor, half-hysterical in his anger. He turned and shot a question:

"Who is with Reynolds?"

"Rios."

"All right — I can depend on him."

"How about cleanin' up the job and pullin' out?" asked Steen.

"Getting yellow, eh?" sneered Bladen. "We don't do a thing, until we get Sontag. Go and find Scott. I'll cut his damn ears off."

"You wasn't so smart," said Steen. "I told yuh to never give Sontag a chance. You thought he was fool enough to fall for yore ideas, didn't yuh? You thought he'd ride north and get cut down by five or six rifles.

He knew what it was all about, and don'tcha forgit it. If you'd taken my advice, he'd never have come out of the cellar. What is five thousand measly dollars in this game? You shore offered him big odds, Bladen."

Bladen did not waste his breath in a reply, but helped himself to a big drink of liquor.

Stormy See and Tiny Parker listened to what Johnny Caldwell and Hewie Moore had to say, and decided to find out a few things. Fowler offered to ride with them, so they went back seven strong.

"I'm not actin' in a legal way," explained Stormy. "But right now I'm a cowman — not a sheriff."

"You never was much of a sheriff," said Tiny, "so yuh ain't hurtin' anythin'."

They circled far wide of the Rios ranch and came in from the north side of the big washout. It was just sundown when they reached the string of horses.

"There's nothin' like playin' safe," said Johnny. "Let's swipe the whole bunch, *cache* the saddles and turn the broncs loose."

Fifteen minutes later twelve loose horses, minus saddles and bridles, went galloping down a swale toward the south, hidden from the Circle R ranch. The seven riders were bunched, watching the disappearing herd of horses, when they heard the first shot fired at the Circle R. It was immediately followed by a second shot.

"That sounds interestin'," remarked Stormy. "Mebbe we better git where we can take a look at things over there."

They were riding slowly back, when the third shot sounded. This was muffled from being fired inside the stable, but was audible.

They came back to the deep washout, where they paused to think it over.

"Our best bet is to cross over and come out on top of that slope over there," said Johnny. "That'll give us a clear view of the place."

"Let's not be too hasty," said Hewie. "Lotsa things to consider. If they come to git their horses, we've got to rattle our hocks out of there awful fast, or they'll see us. Mebbe we better circle around to the right and come in on that ridge to the west of the house. If I remember right there's plenty brush on it."

As they started to go back to their horses, Johnny snapped a warning. Two men had topped the slope, coming toward them, running awkwardly in their high-heel boots. They came down over the opposite edge and into the willows out of sight. Two minutes later they were stumbling back in sight, hurrying to inform the rest of the gang that their horses were gone

"We'll try that west ridge." decided Johnny. "C'mon, gang."

There was consternation in the ranch-house when the two men came panting in to tell them that the horses were gone. It took the heart out of those cowboys, caused them to realize their position.

"Sontag took 'em, jist as sure as hell," wailed one of the two men. "He'll circle back to Singin' River, and we'll have the whole damn valley on our necks."

222

Bladen struck the man on the side of the head with a whisky bottle, knocking the man flat on his face.

"No quitters wanted," he said coldly. "They've got nothing on us."

"With what Sontag knows — they have," said Steen "We won't dare burn the place now, so our best bet is to take 'em out and to a safe place, Doc."

"And not a horse to be had?" queried Bladen. "Don't be a fool. It will be dark within an hour."

"Have a little sense, Doc.," wailed Terrill. "Sontag will bring a posse. He'd go through hell for that pardner of his. I'm no quitter, but I've got enough brains to know when to git out. We can't fight 'em and expect to win — and we can't make a run for it. If we set fire to this place — aw, use yore brains, Doc. The world wouldn't be big enough to hold us."

Farraday had kept in the background until now. He saw Bladen's hand creep back to his pocket, and knew Bladen would kill Terrill.

"Stop it, Doc., he said sternly. "You've bungled as a leader. Keep yore hand away from that gun. That's better. You're goin' to listen to sense or I'll drill you so damn full of holes that they can't pick yuh up in one piece."

Bladen smiled sourly. "Go ahead, Jim. Without me, not a damn one of yuh can collect a cent. You won't shoot your future financial agent."

"Yore scheme went hay-wire," said Farraday. "Sontag throwed a monkey-wrench in yore machinery, Bladen. Right now, it ain't a question of how much money can we collect — but how much life have we got ahead."

"So you are yellow, too, eh?" sneered Bladen.

"You'd be yellow, if yuh wasn't full of dope."

"All this talkin' don't get us anythin'," complained Terrill. "Sontag never seen the face of one of us. He couldn't prove who we were."

"That might be true, but I'd hate to depend on it," replied Farraday. "I wish somebody would find Scott. What in hell became of him, anyway? Did he turn yellow and pull out on us."

"Not that jigger," said someone. "He ain't got brains enough to turn yaller. Mebbe he's chasin' Sontag."

"Did anybody think to look in the cellar?" asked Terrill.

Sad had been sitting on the steps, listening as close as possible to the conversation, rather amused at some of it, and hopeful that the whole gang would decide to head for the hills. But at Terrill's mention of the cellar he slipped off the steps.

The dirty lantern was burning very dimly, threatening at any time to go out.

"Hold fast and don't make a move," hissed Sad. "Back against the posts."

Sad still had his mask, which he adjusted, squeezing in against the bottom of the steps at the rear. Someone threw open the trap-door, and lowered a lighted lantern, illuminating Scott's body.

"By God, he's down there!" exclaimed Farraday. "Look out for trouble."

One of the men swung down low, scanning the cellar. But all he could see was the huddled figures at the posts.

224

"It's all right," he told them. "All safe."

They crowded down there without the lantern. No one of them thought to count how many masked men came down. Sad was with them, one of them, and they paid him no heed, as they examined Scott.

"Socked on the head," said Terrill. "No use takin' him out — he's ridin' on a cloud right now."

"Shovelin' brimstone," corrected another.

"Well, that accounts for Scott," sighed Farraday. "Renn and Scott both gone."

They all climbed out of the cellar, and Sad was surprised to note how dark it was getting. Only one lamp had been lighted, and the room was large. Sad hunkered down against the wall as far as possible from the lamp, while Bladen, Terrill and Farraday discussed the situation.

A man came in from outside, and Sad recognized him as being Lentz, from the Flying M.

"Somebody out there to the west," he said hoarsely. "Out in the brush on that slope. I dunno how many. They're in the brush."

"Are yuh sure of that?" asked Farraday anxiously.

"Sure as hell. I seen at least three of 'em. I've been watchin' 'em for thirty minutes, waitin' to be sure."

"Trapped!" snorted Terrill. "Horses gone and we're surrounded."

"Mebbe not," said Farraday hopefully "If they're only on one —"

"If we wasn't surrounded, why would they lay quiet that-away. I tell yuh, we're surrounded. Sontag went to town and —"

"He hasn't had time," interrupted Bladen. "Lentz is seeing things."

"All right," said Lentz. "When your damn neck is inside a noose, you'll think the sheriff is kiddin' yuh, Doc."

Bladen turned away, his shoulders sagging, and someone laughed.

"I'm sorry," said Bladen softly. "It's all my fault. Do as you please, it doesn't matter to me now. But," he whirled suddenly, a Colt automatic .45 in his hand, "I'll do as I damn please!" he gritted.

They were taken by surprise, and Bladen's keen eyes watched them like a hawk, as the big gun swung in a short arc. Suddenly he shifted the muzzle and the gun spat three times at a pile of stuff in the corner near him; something that was covered with a tarpaulin.

But the big gun was right back, covering them.

"That damn kerosene!" blurted Farraday. The smell was unmistakable now. Those big bullets had bored through the five gallon cans, and it was spreading all around.

"Don't move," warned Bladen. "Don't move. I came here to do a job, and I'm going to do it."

The air was rank with the smell of kerosene now, as it ran in rivulets along the floor. The men watched it as though fascinated. Bladen reached cautiously in his pocket and drew out a handful of matches.

"Don't do that, Doc.," panted Farraday. "Don'tcha know there's a bunch of men out there in the hills that —"

"Shut up, damn yuh!" warned Bladen. "I'd jist as soon leave you here to roast —"

He reached down to scratch the matches on the floor, when Sontag drew and fired. It was probably the fastest draw he ever made in his life, and the most necessary. Bladen's hand halted short of the floor, the matches sifted from his nerveless fingers. Then he slowly slid forward on his face.

CHAPTER
NINETEEN

The sheriff and his men out on the slope had been trying hard to get some sort of a line on the place. There was no sign of activity. As far as they could see the place was deserted. Of course, they were on the doorless side of the building.

"Goin' to be too dark to see anythin' pretty soon," said Tony.

"There's somethin'!" exclaimed Johnny. A man had appeared around the rear of the house, a man without hat or coat. He darted low over the wire fence, wriggled under it and came running up through the brush, as though making a short-cut across the hills to pick up the road to Singing River.

Quickly the seven men spread out to intercept him, and he almost ran into Johnny and Stormy, who promptly covered him with their guns.

It was Dan Reynolds, looking like anything more than a Sheep King. He stopped short, panting heavily. The rest of the posse closed in on them. Fowler grunted softly:

"Mr. Reynolds again, eh?"

Reynolds tried to smile, but it was only the grimace of a tired old man. They did not need to question him

— he told. Swiftly he sketched out what was going on in the Circle R ranch-house, while they looked at him in amazement.

"I was going to find help," he told them. "Dell Rios let me go to get help."

"And they didn't kill Sontag?" asked Johnny.

"No. As near as I could learn, Sontag fooled them, shot Renn, and got Renn's mask. They thought he was Renn, and he got back to the house, where he — I don't know what he did to Scott. They can't find him. And their horses are all gone.

Suddenly they heard the three shots from Bladen's automatic. Stormy grinned.

"They're fightin' it out among themselves. What's left we'll finish. Let's go down, boys."

"Let me have a gun," begged Reynolds. "Remember, I've got a son down there."

Stormy drew out a six-shooter, looked keenly at Reynolds and said:

"Yo're the first shepherd that ever got a gun off me, Reynolds; I'm takin' a chance."

Then came the heavier detonation of Sad's big six-shooter, and the eight men spread out and went quickly down toward the house.

Lentz and Bowers were outside, trying to locate more of the surrounding posse, when Sad shot Bladen. They saw the men coming down through the brush, and got back into the house not more than ten seconds after Bladen had sprawled into the kerosene he had intended to set fire to the house. No one made a move, until they came in.

"They're closin' in on us!" yelled Lentz. "Damn it, let's make a break and fight it out in the open."

And this was no orderly procession. The men made a rush for the kitchen doorway, crowding, fighting to get out of that house. Sad did not join in the exodus. He saw Steen race up the stairs and heard him slam a door.

Sad, wondering why Steen went up the stairs, stepped just outside the kitchen doorway, tearing off his mask. He saw Farraday whirl and fire one shot, and then it seemed as though something cut him off at the knees. Lentz was down on his hands and knees.

He saw Terrill get hit, go to his knees, get up and throw both hands above his head. Rifles were cracking merrily. Sad heard Steen running down the stairs. He stepped aside, as Steen ran out he flung out a foot and sent him sprawling, his gun flying out of his hand.

Steen turned on his side and looked back into the muzzle of Sad's six-shooter, and the long, lean face behind it was smiling.

"Don't move, Steen," he warned. "I'd hate to kill yuh, but I'd do it in a minute."

Stormy See ran in past the corner, stuffing shells into the loading gate of his rifle. Johnny Caldwell, at the front porch, was yelling to Hewie to quit shooting, because everybody wanted to surrender. Slim and Tony were running along the fence, covering a group of men with their rifles, warning them to not make any false moves.

Stormy stopped and stared at Sad and his captive.

"How are yuh, Stormy?" asked Sad.

"Damn sight wiser than I was, Sontag. Man, what a cleanup!"

Dan Reynolds came around the corner, walking wearily, an empty six-shooter in his hand. He looked at Sad and tried to smile, he said:

"Well, we meet again, Sontag."

"Looks thataway," said Sad, a bit mystified. "Stormy, go and help the boys, but send Johnny up here."

"Where the hell do you fit into this?" asked Steen, glaring at Dan Reynolds.

"Oh, I just got away from Rios."

Johnny came running, and handed Sad a short piece of rope, which Sad handed to Reynolds and indicated Steen.

"Tie him up for me, will yuh, Reynolds?" and then to Johnny:

"The trap-door in the kitchen, Johnny. Open it up and yell who yuh are — they're armed."

Then he watched Reynolds tie Steen's hands tightly. The sheriff and his men were marching the captives up to the house. Farraday, Lentz, Terrill and Bowers were unable to be moved. There were only four unharmed prisoners, Smeed and Harlow from the Lazy N Half Circle R, and Meeker and Wheeler from the Box A A. Sneed was supposed to be the owner of the Lazy N Half Circle R. The rest were merely hired men, sick of their job and glad to quit.

"Any casualties in the yard?" asked Sad.

"Four cripples," panted Stormy. "God, what a evenin'!"

Johnny had opened the cellar, and now he came out with Jean, Gale and Swede. Jean was crying, and Swede was swearing, because he never had any hand in the fighting. Gale looked as though he was about to collapse, until he saw his father. They looked keenly at each other for several moments.

"Shake hands with him, Gale," yelled Johnny. "He got away and came to get help."

"You got away?" queried Gale. "Did they have you too, Dad?"

"Somebody bring Dell Rios down from upstairs," ordered Reynolds. "He let me tie him up and slide out of the window. You see, I was slated to take my last look at things to-night. Bladen — what happened to him?"

"He hit the hot spot," replied Smeed. "Damn fool, he tried to burn up the place."

"Yo're Smeed, ain't yuh?" asked Sad, and Smeed nodded.

"How much did Reynolds know about yore outfit and the Box A A rustlin' Two Bar J P and Bar 44 cattle?"

Smeed looked keenly at Sad, shifted his eyes to Reynolds, and shrugged his shoulders.

"As long as yuh know it — nothin'. Terrill, Farraday, Steen, Rios, Ellis, me and my gang and Renn and his gang were in on it. You'll find Ellis at the Flyin' M. Steen killed him last night, because Ellis wanted to quit and go south."

Slim and Tony came out with Dell Rios. The owner of the Circle R did not look like a criminal, but his eyes shifted quickly, when he saw Jean looking at him.

"I may be rather out of place in this," said Reynolds, "but I want to say a few words. Dell Rios was forced into this. Remember the day Jean Proctor's father was killed? He was murdered. Steen was working for me. Proctor and Rios got into an argument in the corral, and Proctor tried to knock Rios down.

"In protecting himself, Rios knocked Proctor down against the fence, cutting his scalp. Rios was frightened and ran to the house to get some cold water — and Steen finished the job with a pick-handle. Rios didn't know it. When he came back Proctor was dead. We held it as a club over Rios. He was afraid to not obey us.

"Rios even came to San Francisco to shoot me. He intended to wipe me out, come back and kill Steen — and play square with the rest of you. I'm telling you this, hoping you'll understand. I'm willing to get on the stand and swear to everything I've told you."

The men stood around in silence. Jean was crying again and Johnny was trying to comfort her. Steen, white-faced, read no mercy in the faces around him.

"Let the law have him," said Sad. "It won't show him many favors, not with a Singin' River jury. Somebody git the horses, so we can take the cripples to a doctor."

"And when that is done," said Reynolds, "I want some of you boys to ride with me."

"Ride where?" asked Slim.

"To meet the sheep over beyond the rim tomorrow morning — and turn them back to Sunset. I'm all through with sheep — and so is Singing River Valley, as far as I can prevent it."

"That sounds mighty nice to me," said Uncle Hewie.

"And every head of Box A A and Lazy N Half Circle R stock goes back to their original owners."

"Why don'tcha run the Flyin' M yourself?" asked Sad. "Raisin' cows ain't a bad business."

"I — I don't think I'm wanted around here — not after what I've done."

"There's a lot of us livin' in glass houses," said Stormy.

"I wish you would, Dad," said Gale. "Cow folks are regular."

"Who killed old Lightnin'?" demanded Slim.

"Steen," said Rios.

"Too bad he didn't last a couple years more, he might have built up quite a reputation," said Swede, as they went down to help load up the cripples.

They could see Jean and Johnny together at the kitchen door, Gale and his father at the corner of the porch. It was too dark to see them very plain. Johnny was saying something about going to tell Jean something she *ought* to believe, and Dan Reynolds was patting Gale on the arm and trying to explain things.

Someone brought a lantern and they finished taking care of the wounded. Hewie came up to Sad and held out his hand.

"Sontag, shake hands with the biggest fool in the valley," said the old man. "I can't give yuh the Bar 44, 'cause it's in my wife's name; but I can make yuh foreman, if you'll accept."

"I was thinking seriously of turning the Flying M over to him," interrupted Reynolds, who came up behind them.

"Sad!" It was Jean calling him. "Come here, Sad."

"Excuse me," laughed Sad, and walked back to them. Johnny grasped Sad by the arm, while Jean did the talking.

"Sad Sontag, will you accept the job as foreman of the Two Bar J P? I want you both — you and Swede. Will you take it, Sad — please?"

Sad grinned in the darkness. "Well, I'll tell yuh, Jean — it kinda looks as though yuh had a perfectly good foreman right with yuh. Johnny Caldwell knows cows and he's —"

"Are you meanin' the half owner of the Two Bar J P?" drawled Johnny.

"An owner always needs a good foreman," added Jean.

"Great lovely dove!" exploded Sad. He nearly hugged both of them, jerked away and headed back for the stable, where he met Stormy.

"I'm sendin' to town for more horses," Stormy told him. "We'll need a wagon to haul in the cripples and the casualties. Man, you must have kinda worked on 'em before we ever got here. How didja ever do it. Farraday told me yuh had the bunch whipped, before we ever got into it. You must have talked fast."

"I did," said Sad wearily.

"And big words, eh?" grunted Stormy appreciatively.

"Yeah, big ones, Stormy — with lead overcoats on. I told yuh I was goin' to talk in a language they'd understand. But it was all right — I got my pardner back."

"And saved the valley from rustlers and sheep."

"And that," said Sad slowly, "is what they call in a factory — a by-product."

"My gosh," grunted Tiny, puffing up to them. "What a job — and the worst is yet to come."

"What do yuh mean?" asked Stormy anxiously.

"Explainin' this in detail to my wife. Lordy, how I wish I could be Swedish for an hour."

Sad turned back and found Swede talking with Jean and Johnny.

"Swede accepts," said Jean happily. "I explained things to him, and he accepts."

"Well," Sad laughed softly, his hand on Swede's shoulder, "I've always gone where my pardner goes — even into cellars. I reckon you've got two hired hands."

They were silent as the tip of the moon silvered the hills around them. Somewhere, far out in the hills, a coyote wailed mournfully. From the ridge of the old house a mockingbird called sleepily.

"I'm glad you came to Singing River, Sad Sontag," said Jean.

"Yeah, it's a good place to come, Jean," he replied.

"Even if we all tried hard to run you out?"

Sad laughed softly. "I reckon Singin' River Valley is a whole lot like they tell us about Heaven. Hard place for a strange cowpuncher to git into, but a good place for to live."

"She's sure jist like Heaven to me." said Johnny.

"You wouldn't even know the difference, if the whole darn place was on fire," laughed Swede. "C'mon, Sad, let's go talk to sensible folks."

And they wandered away in the darkness together.